# THE SURVIVORS

# THE
# SURVIVORS

## GEORGES SIMENON

Translated from the French
by Stuart Gilbert

A Helen and Kurt Wolff Book
Harcourt Brace Jovanovich, Publishers
San Diego   New York   London

LIBRARY OF CONGRESS CATALOGING IN PUBLICATION DATA

Simenon, Georges, 1903–
The survivors.

Translation of: Les rescapés du Télémaque.
Reprint. Originally published: Boston: Routledge &
Kegan Paul, 1965.
"A Helen and Kurt Wolff book."
I. Title.
PQ2637.I53R4513    1985      843'.912      84–22385
ISBN 0–15–187047–0

*Designed by Mark Likgalter*

Printed in the United States of America

First American edition 1985

A B C D E

# THE
# SURVIVORS

# 1

LIKE CAUSES have effects, and the coming of a boat to port involves a series of activities much the same the world over, even though the boat in question be a mere Fécamp trawler equipped for herring fishing. Indeed, it wouldn't have been worthwhile mentioning the events preceding the *Centaur*'s arrival but for one circumstance that was exceptional.

Needless to say, everyone knew of her approach well before the boat herself showed on the horizon. There was the vaguest glimmer, no more than a hint of daybreak, in the east; it was that uncertain moment when one can say neither that day is dawning nor that the night persists. Far out in the offing a masthead light swayed and flickered above the heaving darkness of the Channel.

At the Café de l'Amiral shutters were up, lamps lighted inside, chairs still stacked on tables, and a black pail dripping soapsuds held the middle of the tiled floor. Jules, the owner, shouted to his servant:

"Hurry up, Babette! The *Centaur*'ll be in within the hour."

And Babette, who was kneeling on the tiles, her feet in clogs, her sodden apron clinging to her slender hips, looked up; then, tossing back her shock of reddish curls, she began to ply her rag in wider sweeps.

In the big house on the quay, facing the railway siding, Monsieur Pessart the shipowner was already up and about, shaved and dressed. He was straightening his tie as he stepped into the dining room, where a girl about Babette's age, but as dark as Babette was fair, was setting out cups and plates on a tablecloth spotted here and there with wine.

One couldn't yet be sure if the sun had risen; another of those dark days was beginning, when lights have to be kept on until noon. It had been the same on the previous day except for a weak attempt at sunshine toward eleven in the morning.

Nor could one say with any more certainty whether the moisture on the cobblestones and the men's coats was due to a light drizzle or to spray from the breakers crashing on the beach with the steady rumble of a barrage.

Anyhow, the weather was no worse than usual for the time of year. Women could be seen hurrying into groceries and butcher shops; their husbands would be back in an hour or so, clamoring for a warm meal, and the shopkeepers knew that, later in the morning, the women would be dropping in again to settle their bills.

All this, of course, was quite normal; as it always was when a herring boat came in. And there was the usual procession of fishwives wheeling handcarts down to the dock, where they'd soon start unloading. Also as usual, Jules, the owner of the Café de l'Amiral, was standing beside the big coffee urn, drawing for himself the first cup, while Babette, her hair tumbling over her eyes, slammed chairs and tables into place.

What made the difference on this morning was the presence of four men at the Normandie, a hotel mainly patronized by traveling salesmen; four men who, while they ate their rolls and butter, kept their eyes fixed on the harbor mouth.

2

It is usually hard to say at what precise moment a town wakes up. At Fécamp, however, one could have fixed it almost to the minute on this particular morning. All of a sudden one heard carts rattling down to the waterfront, engines whistling at the station, cars tooting at corners; and a moment later the black mass of the *Centaur* loomed up in the fairway between the long arms of the jetties.

At the extreme end of one of these stood Monsieur Pessart, a bulky form outlined against the grayness. He was wearing polished clogs, black gaiters, and a dark overcoat. So far he had not been seen to speak to anyone, yet somehow word had gone around that he wanted the *Centaur* to start out again at once, with the turn of the tide.

This was the chief topic of conversation at Jules's café, where Babette, having taken off her apron, was tidying herself up in front of a wall mirror, while fumes of coffee laced with brandy began to fill the air.

"They'll refuse to go out, mark my words," Jules declared. He was wearing a thick sweater of the kind affected by bicycle racers. "And I don't blame 'em," he added.

The newspapers had stories of a Greek tramp foundering in the North Sea, of a collier in difficulties off La Pallice. The *Bremen* had made New York twenty hours late.

So steep were the seas even in the harbor mouth that sometimes the hull of the *Centaur* disappeared completely, then rose so high that it seemed about to swoop upon the dock.

The four men staying at the Normandie had moved down to the waterfront. The air was raw, and they had their hands thrust deep in their overcoat pockets. At first sight one would have taken them for casual onlookers, such as always gather on a quay to watch a ship come in. Indeed, with their felt hats and blue overcoats, they had the look of businessmen on holiday.

Signals were exchanged between the men on the

3

trawler's deck and those on shore; handkerchiefs were waved. Cautiously the *Centaur* edged her way alongside.

A hatless woman asked the young railwayman standing beside her: "I've heard he wants them to go out again next tide. Know anything about it?"

There were a number of people gathered around Monsieur Pessart, but he spoke to no one and continued sucking at the black cigar that rarely left his lips and was never lighted; his doctor had forbidden him to smoke.

A mooring rope slapped on the cobblestones. The smell of fish grew stronger, and the four men from the hotel began to push their way to the front.

While the crew were making fast, Monsieur Pessart, without worrying whether his clothes got dirty, swung himself over the rail and went up to Pierre Canut, his skipper, who was dressed exactly like his crew, in yellow oilskins and rubber boots.

A woman shouted to her husband, who was dragging a hawser along the deck: "He wants you to put out again at once, with the tide."

The man scowled. "Have no fear!"

It was the usual story; when, as now, the herring shoal was exceptionally large—this had been announced on the radio—the owners of the boats refused to lose a single day, even a tide. This meant that the crews, after ten or twelve days at sea, had only just time enough to rush home for a change of clothes before starting out again. It was worse for those who lived in the outlying villages—Les Loges, Bénouville, Vauxcottes; they didn't even have time to see their wives and children. Instead, they hurried to the shops and came back laden with provisions for another ten or twelve days at sea.

"That's what *you* say. But he'll talk you into it."

Canut could be seen on deck in earnest talk with Monsieur Pessart, and some bolder spirit shouted to him from the dock: "Don't let him bluff you, Pierre. Courage!"

Canut swung around, and his blue eyes settled on the speaker. He had his usual expression of imperturbable good humor, but now he scratched his head—a sure sign, with him, that he was about to take a stand. But before he could say anything, the four strangers, to whom nobody had paid much attention, climbed on board the trawler, taking care not to soil their clothes, and started talking with Canut and the *Centaur*'s owner. They formed so odd a group that everyone began to stare, trying to make out what was happening.

Canut's first movement had been to take a quick step backward, like someone whose toes have been stepped on. But he was always inclined to be jerky in his movements. Monsieur Pessart, however, was showing signs of agitation and shifting the unlit cigar from one side of his mouth to the other.

Meanwhile, casks of herrings were being hauled out of the holds and loaded on the carts, while coal rattled down an iron chute into the bunkers.

"What do they want with your brother?" someone asked the young man in railway uniform.

"Haven't any idea."

Charles Canut was about to go on board when one of the four men stepped quickly forward and barred his way.

"No one's allowed here, now. Soon."

"But . . ."

"There's no 'but' about it."

That was surprising enough, but even more surprising was the behavior of Monsieur Pessart, ordinarily the most self-controlled of men. He had suddenly started gesticulating—in broad daylight, too, with half the town looking on. And a moment later he stepped off the boat, shouting angrily: "I won't stand for it! I'm going to see the mayor."

He pushed his way through the crowd, muttering to himself.

The crowd had nearly an hour to wait before learning

what the trouble was. During this time, two of the strangers were seen going to the police station, accompanied by Canut, while the other two men kept guard on the *Centaur*'s deck.

When Canut reappeared, everyone was struck by his appearance. He had an almost hangdog air; all his self-assurance had gone. Indeed, one woman remarked as he passed her that he looked "like death warmed over."

His brother hurried toward him. "Pierre! What's happening?"

But Canut merely shrugged his shoulders, seeming to mean that he could make nothing of it, or else that there was nothing to be done.

To save time, Monsieur Pessart had sent his car, which now drew up on the dock. In it were the mayor and the president of the Federation of Shipowners.

There was another conversation on board the *Centaur*. It seemed that the most important-looking of the four strangers was patiently repeating: "I've no say in the matter. I'm only carrying out my orders."

At that moment, Monsieur Pessart, ordinarily so taciturn, turned toward the crowd and exclaimed in a voice rough with indignation: "They want to take Captain Canut to jail!"

The remark was addressed to everyone and to no one in particular; to all who lived by or on the sea—that is, to everyone present with the exception of the four landsmen in blue coats.

Things looked bad. The crew of the *Centaur* pressed from all sides to the front of the crowd, making a menacing half-circle of yellow oilskins and grim, unshaven faces.

"Gentlemen," began the police superintendent. There was a note of anxiety in his voice.

"Throw him overboard!" a woman yelled.

Pushing aside the man whe barred his way to the deck, Charles Canut went up to his brother.

"Pierre! What is it?"

Of them all, it was Pierre who seemed the calmest. He was scratching his head under his cap, sometimes gazing at the deck and sometimes at the people around him.

Monsieur Pessart was arguing with the superintendent. "You've no right to stop my ship from going out, under the circumstances. There's no other skipper available in Fécamp. I wonder if you realize the heavy financial loss for all concerned if you persist in this high-handed conduct."

The mayor looked worried. The crowd showed signs of turning nasty, and he was wondering if he shouldn't send for more police.

"Perhaps," he suggested, "you could see your way to questioning Canut on the spot, in which case . . ."

"Sorry, but I have orders to take him to Rouen and hand him over to the examining magistrate."

"And if I vouch for him?"

"I am sorry, but . . ."

From the dock came an angry buzz of voices.

"Canut," said the superintendent, "in your own interest, I advise you to leave quietly. I have a warrant for your arrest, and if you or your friends offer any resistance, you will regret it."

The most surprising thing was that Canut, quick-tempered as he was at normal times for all his good-humored air, should be taking it so calmly, that he hadn't lashed out at the superintendent and the other men. He looked bored and ill at ease, no more than that, as he shifted his weight from one foot to the other, and when he turned his eyes toward the people on the dock, he hardly seemed to recognize them.

They were lined up three or four deep alongside the *Centaur*, and more were coming all the time, from all parts of town. Jules had wormed his way to the front row; Babette was watching from the doorway of the inn.

"I suggest, gentlemen, that we adjourn to the town hall, and I'll telephone the public prosecutor at Rouen. I'm sure something can be arranged."

It went off without trouble; that is, the little group of men was allowed to disembark in peace and way was made for them to pass. But once they were through, the crowd streamed after them in a ragged procession toward the town hall.

Charles Canut followed with the others. He and his skipper brother were twins. Both had gone to sea as boys, but Charles, whose lungs were weak, had had to give up the sea and take a less exacting job on shore.

Pierre Canut walked in front, accompanied by the superintendent and his inspectors, who had refrained from handcuffing him. The shipowner and the local officials discussed the situation as they drove to the town hall in Monsieur Pessart's car.

"It's utterly absurd, this charge they're making against Canut: that he killed old Février. And, in any case, when a ship is due to go to sea, I'm pretty sure they have no right to hold her up."

On arriving at the town hall, everyone was surprised to see the clock pointing to ten. Time had passed more quickly than they'd realized.

Now and again the superintendent took his watch from his pocket. "Let me remind you that we must leave by the eleven-thirteen, without fail."

Canut, the inspectors, the president of the Federation of Shipowners, and Monsieur Pessart entered the mayor's office, whose padded door was slammed in Charles Canut's face.

"Give me the public prosecutor of Rouen, please . . . Yes, it's very urgent."

Here, too, lamps were lighted; and a smell of fish hung in the air, as it does in every part of Fécamp.

"Tell me the truth, Canut. Did you really . . . ?" The mayor's voice was almost pleading.

"No, sir. I did *not* kill Monsieur Février."

"Then why should they arrest you?"

"I haven't any idea."

8

The police began to lose patience.

"Let me tell you," said the superintendent, "that a thorough inquiry was made before this step was taken. Monsieur Laroche, the examining magistrate in charge of the case, went into all the facts most carefully."

Though the windows were shut, one couldn't help being conscious of the crowd outside. Not that there was any uproar; on the contrary, they were surprisingly quiet. But the sound of the shuffling feet and the murmur of many voices conveyed a sense of menace, like the rumble of an impending storm.

"I see your point, Superintendent. But I happen to know that the Canut brothers are held in high esteem in Fécamp—Pierre among the seamen and his brother among all our townsfolk. Just go to that window and take a look."

More people had come, and by now there were fully five hundred men and women, all of them gazing up at the window of the mayor's office. The mayor was at the telephone.

"Yes, it's I, the mayor of Fécamp." And the mayor explained his difficulty. "I can assure you . . . What's that you say? . . . But I can give you my most solemn assurance that . . . What? . . . In that case, I beg your pardon. . . . Very well then. I regret having troubled you, but I was motivated, as I trusted you understand, by my obligations to the public interest—and my conscience."

This was one of his pet phrases and had served in many perorations; on this occasion he uttered it with genuine feeling.

"Yes, yes. I quite understand. And you can count on my taking the necessary steps."

Actually, he was seething with indignation, but he preferred to keep an appearance of calm and dignity in the presence of these outsiders, whose powers were so superior to his own. He turned to the police.

"Under the circumstances, gentlemen, I have nothing

9

further to say. You can take away your prisoner. As the chief authority in this town, I shall take steps to see that there is no trouble of any kind. I shall post our local police force at the main entrance and have my car waiting for you in the small street at the back. One of my staff will show you the way. I advise you not to take the train at Fécamp, but to drive on to La Bréauté, the next station, where you can catch the Havre express.

"Good day to you, gentlemen. As for you, Canut, I trust that all will go well and we will see you back among us very soon. I regret, Monsieur Pessart, that I can do nothing for you. I look to you to do your best to calm down public feeling and, above all, to do nothing that might lead to a breach of the peace."

So it was over. Pierre Canut was in custody.

Perhaps he was the only one who failed to realize the gravity of his position; indeed, his friends were puzzled by his almost indifferent manner. It passed their understanding how a man of his kind, who at the age of thirty-three was regarded as one of the best skippers on the coast, could take a thing like this so apathetically.

The crowd, meanwhile, was growing restive, and even within the four walls of the mayor's office one felt the tension in the air. At one time it seemed that the sounds outside grew louder, and the mayor hastened to the window, followed by Police Superintendent Gentil.

There was something both grotesque and tragic in what they saw. A woman in her fifties, dressed in black, was roaming to and fro with oddly jerky steps, accosting members of the crowd. Though all the people she approached drew back at once, she went on speaking to them, in a low, singsong voice, as if talking to herself. She showed no surprise when they refused to listen; evidently she was used to this. Slowly, mournfully, she went her way, with steps as measured as a sleepwalker's.

"Who is it?" the superintendent asked in a low voice.

And the mayor, bending toward him, whispered: "His mother."

Canut must have overheard, because he raised his head abruptly. But he did not cross the five yards between himself and the window; he merely frowned.

In the street, Charles Canut took his mother's arm and steered her out of the crowd, while she continued her interminable monologue for him alone.

In answer to the superintendent's questioning look, the mayor tapped his brow with his forefinger. Then everyone turned toward the door; an employee had come to say that the car was waiting in the back street.

The superintendent had no satisfaction in doing it, but it seemed best to be on the safe side, especially when one had to deal with a man standing six feet in his socks and measuring over forty inches around the chest. With a deft movement, he clicked the handcuffs on Canut's wrists, saying almost apologetically: "I'm acting under instructions." To which he added after a moment: "I'd have allowed you to go home for a change of clothes and to get your things; but with all those people outside, I can't take any risks. Anyhow, you can arrange with your family to send whatever you need."

The mayor's chauffeur drove the closed car along a road bordered by black, sodden fields.

"Unless, of course . . ." the police superintendent now added; but he left the phrase unfinished.

Unless, he meant, Canut was set at liberty that evening. But no one seemed to anticipate this; not even Canut, who was frowning, like a man brooding on unwelcome thoughts.

As usual, there was quite a crowd on the platform at La Bréauté. At first, no one noticed the handcuffs, but presently the little group had to move to the far end of the platform to escape curious eyes. The yellow oilskins, especially, seemed to attract attention.

There was no empty compartment, and they had to travel with two elderly gentlemen, who seemed unable to take their eyes off the prisoner. No one spoke, but the silence was heavy with unspoken thoughts. The windows were clouded with steam, and the train was insufferably hot for a man dressed for the high winds of the open sea.

Meanwhile, at Fécamp feelings were running high. The crowd showed no sign of dispersing, though the mayor in person positively assured them that Canut had left the town hall by the back door. To make things worse, someone had spread a rumor that Monsieur Pessart had telephoned to Boulogne for another skipper to take the *Centaur* to sea.

By noon there were so many people in the Café de l'Amiral that it was impossible to see the tables. Babette was looking rather pale, though there were red patches on her cheeks, due to the effort needed to make her way between the customers, serve drinks, and retrieve empty glasses. She was a focus of interest, and now and again someone would ask her: "What has your fiancé to say about it?"

She would give an impatient toss of her head that sent wisps of red-gold hair straggling across her freckled face. She was engaged to Charles, Pierre Canut's twin brother, who spent all his evenings in a corner of the café, where Babette sat with him whenever she had a moment off.

"How should I know?" was her reply.

There were oilskins and ordinary overcoats, sailors ready to go to sea and others who, not being employed on herring boats, had many weeks ahead on land.

One of the latter bawled from a corner of the café: "You won't let yourselves be bossed by some fellow from Boulogne, will you?"

Not they! They thumped the tables, swearing they'd be damned before they worked under any other skipper; they'd wait till Canut was back.

Some of the men had their wives with them. The air was steamy, full of smoke and brandy fumes. Waves of heat came from the stove and an icy draft swept the room whenever the door was opened.

"Why should Canut have killed him? It don't make sense."

Nip followed nip. One began by ordering a glass of coffee laced with brandy, then, when halfway through, one had a second nip poured in. After that, when the glass was empty but still warm, one ordered another laced coffee. And as the brandy took effect, speech grew thicker and indignation rose.

"Pierre's the best skipper in Fécamp, and that's as good as saying the best in the whole of France—and I defy any-one to deny it."

"The he is, and we won't sail without him, will we?"

"Not us!"

"What beats me is why we didn't bash their mugs in while we were about it."

One of Monsieur Pessart's clerks entered the café and informed them that a captain from Boulogne would be arriving at two and the *Centaur* was to leave with the next tide.

There was a chorus of protests; nothing, they told the clerk, would induce them to sail under another skipper. But presently one of the crew went quietly out to buy his provisions for the voyage; then another; then another. After all, when one has a wife, and kids . . .

"If it doesn't sail today, he'll lay her up. That's what he said, anyhow."

Which made them scratch their heads.

Then someone remarked: "Queer, ain't it? Canut didn't even try to stand up to them."

"Suppose he really killed that fellow . . . ?"

It had begun on a heroic note, and the mayor had even sent for extra police in case things took a dangerous turn. A meeting of the local shipowners had been hurriedly convened, and they had been on the point of begging Monsieur Pessart to refrain from ordering the *Centaur* out.

Nevertheless, at four o'clock, when night was falling and all one could see of the harbor was some specks of light, white, green, and red, through the drizzle, a big lamp with a reflector was lighting up the *Centaur*'s deck and hatches were being made fast.

At the Amiral men gulped down a final brandy before tramping heavily down the dock.

"Have you seen him?"

"What's he look like?"

They were referring to the new skipper, of whom they'd hardly had a glimpse so far. Anyhow, they'd show him the stuff that Fécamp men were made of!

A few women lingered on the misty dock to watch the trawler dwindle into the darkness and climb the black slope of the first big wave beyond the jetties.

Only at six o'clock could Charles Canut leave the freight station where he was employed and settle down in his usual place in Jules's café.

Babette, who looked tired and listless, came up to him after a moment. "What shall I get you?"

It was always the same; he had to order something or other to justify his presence and enable him to profit by the rare occasions when she had no other customers to serve and could sit beside him.

PIERRE HAD been given the usual prisoner's fare: a couple of ham sandwiches and half a bottle of wine. He hardly knew where he was or what was happening. All he knew was that he was waiting; and he went on waiting until five o'clock, at which hour he was led to a poorly lighted but overheated room, where a man in a black coat, seated at a mahogany desk, politely asked him to take a chair.

"You are Pierre Canut, aged thirty-three, son of Pierre

Canut, deceased. You mother's maiden name was Picard. Is that correct?"

Canut was still in handcuffs, but by now he had forgotten about them. A young man was seated at a smaller table and appeared to be writing down what was said.

Monsieur Laroche, the examining magistrate, was a man of forty-five or so, with a small beard of the type worn by the heroes of Jules Verne's stories. He also had the look of scrupulous probity and candor that one associates with those worthies.

The only lamp in the room stood on the desk; it had a green shade, and the light fell on a file of documents, which the magistrate consulted now and again.

"I presume, Canut, that you realize the gravity of the charge on which you have been arrested. That, in fact, is why I have decided to limit your examination today to the question of identity. Once you have engaged a lawyer . . ."

"I don't need a lawyer," said Canut in a calm voice.

"That may be, but I am bound by law to have your lawyer present at your examination."

"But I haven't done anything!"

"So you must either choose a lawyer or the court will appoint one for you. Perhaps I may add that, in your own interest, since you have the means to do so, you'd do better . . ."

"But, sir, I swear to you I didn't kill Monsieur Février."

It was the first time since morning that he showed signs of animation; the first time, too, that a slight flush came to his cheeks, and he seemed conscious of his handcuffs—perhaps because he wanted to raise his arms and accompany his words with gestures.

"I know what you're going to tell me," he continued. "When the superintendent asked me this morning if I'd been to Monsieur Février's house recently, I said no. I didn't know then that he was dead, and I couldn't see what business he had . . ."

"Let me point out, Canut, that I have not put any question to you; in fact, I've warned you not to make any statement at this stage of the proceedings."

Canut merely shrugged his shoulders and continued talking. "The superintendent badgered me with questions, but I stuck to what I'd said. Then he asked me right out if, when we were last on shore—that is, on the night of February the second—I hadn't gone to see Monsieur Février. I can only repeat that then I didn't know, and I was quite justified in thinking that what I'd done or hadn't done was no business of his. So I said no again."

The magistrate turned toward his clerk. "I ask you not to record these statements."

"But you can see the situation I was in. As man to man, I ask you, sir! The superintendent had gone down to my cabin. He'd found the tobacco pouch. So, to cut things short, I told him I'd had it for years."

"Let me remind you, Canut, that your examination must take place in the presence of your lawyer."

"But I don't need one."

"You'll have a lawyer whether you need one or not. That's the law."

"Then when will I have the right to explain things?"

"When a day is fixed by the court for your examination. Meanwhile, by virtue of my functions as examining magistrate, I charge you formally with the murder of Monsieur Emile Février, aged sixty-six, resident at the Villa des Mouettes, Fécamp, at 1:00 A.M. or thereabouts, on February the third, the weapon used being a sailor's jackknife found at the scene of the crime."

Canut shrugged again.

"I also charge you with the theft of money and securities owned by the deceased, as well as other valuables."

At the same moment as the magistrate was charging Canut, the *Centaur* was putting out of Fécamp harbor under the command of a skipper who came from another locality and had never been on the herring run before.

Already she was lifting to the three big waves between the breakwaters.

Night had fallen, and on shore the only lights were those of bistro windows, railway signals of various colors twinkling in the mist, and, spaced through the darkness, infrequent street lamps rimmed with silvery sheen.

THE MAGISTRATE said to his clerk: "Call in the guard and have him taken to his cell."

Canut had held out till the end, and refused to name a lawyer.

The superintendent who had arrested him was playing bridge at the Café de la Comédie. And, at the Amiral, Charles Canut was waiting till Babette could come and sit beside him.

As for Madame Canut, she was saying to her sister, who looked up from her needlework now and again with an anxious expression: "Very soon my dear husband will hear the good news. And when he learns that God has smitten the last of those evildoers . . ." She said such things in a quiet, matter-of-fact tone, without raising her voice or showing any emotion. "I attended that man's funeral, just to make sure. There were four of them in the beginning. Now the last has joined the other three, and my dear one can enter into his peace."

A jet of steam was issuing from the kettle spout, and on a corner of the stove the evening soup was simmering. The Canuts' house was always perfectly kept, without a speck of dust anywhere. In the little-used living room an enlarged photograph hung in the center of one wall. It showed a man of about twenty-four in a sailor's outfit, who, but for his mustache, resembled both his sons, but Charles more markedly than Pierre—Pierre, who now was beginning his first night's sleep in prison.

# 2

CHARLES DID not leave work until six; his brother's plight did not exempt him from his duties at the station. Mechanically, in a sort of dream, he had carried them out, a pencil with an eraser behind his ear.

The day's work ended, he looked in at two cafés, not to drink, but to get in touch with Filloux, a friend of his whom he wanted to replace him at the station the following day. Rain was coming down in torrents, and the lights in the shop windows did little to mitigate the dreariness of the streets. In any case, long, unlighted spaces lay between the shops: pools of darkness into which the passersby seemed to plunge and vanish, though one still heard their voices.

"Hello, Charles!"

He jumped. Not that he was really startled, but he hadn't been expecting to be addressed. Peering through the dark, he recognized his cousin Berthe. Evidently she had been to church; she was carrying a prayer book, and a faint smell of incense lingered around her.

"What are you going to do? I stopped at your house on my way to church. Mama's there now; she heard that Aunt was very upset. Any news of Pierre?"

"No, nothing at all. I'll have to go to Rouen."

"I've just been praying for him. And tomorrow, when I go to High Mass, I shall make my communion for a special intention—on Pierre's behalf."

A pleasant-looking, rosy-cheeked girl, she was the daughter of Madame Lachaume, his mother's sister, who had a pastry shop on Rue d'Etretat.

"Well, good night, Charles. And good luck."

"Good night, Berthe."

He had had a vague intention of going home first, to see his mother. But now that his aunt was with her, and, when she left, Berthe would replace her, this seemed unnecessary. Indeed, there was nothing to prevent his leaving for Rouen at once, since he had found Filloux and made arrangements for the following day.

But the temptation was too strong; he decided to drop in first at the Café de l'Amiral. Throughout the day he'd had no thoughts for anyone but his brother; now he scowled when he saw Paumelle sitting at a table beside the bar and Babette talking to a customer at the far end of the room.

He knew it was absurd, but there was nothing to be done about it. All the time he wasn't actually at the Amiral, he fretted, picturing Babette allowing all sorts of familiarities to the men she served.

"You've no reason to think such things," she told him. "It isn't fair. Why, I'm barely polite to them."

That was so. Jules often reproached her for this, and gave Charles sour looks—as if he were responsible! Still, at times it was impossible for Babette to prevent some of the rougher fishermen from taking liberties, chucking her under the chin or making bawdy remarks.

On this particular evening it was worse than usual, because of Paumelle, a young lout of twenty who never did a stroke of work, but hung around the harbor on the chance of picking up a stray franc by fair means or foul, or getting someone to pay for him. A "wharf rat."

Paumelle made a point of sitting near the bar, as Charles did, but on the other side. How he raised his voice deliberately, to say to Babette: "Give me a box of matches, dear."

It had happened before. Charles had come to have a chat with Babette, and instead of that he had to remain planted at his table, glaring at Paumelle. He had to ask for a drink, too, like an ordinary customer, and Babette had to bring it.

"I forbid you to let that fellow call you 'dear.'"

"Oh, you know he's a sort of cousin—and we were at school together."

"That's neither here nor there. I won't have him talking to you like that."

A number of customers had entered and were clamoring for drinks, so Babette had to leave him. They were the crew of a trawler that had just come in, fifteen or twenty men in oilskins frozen hard as boards.

"Anything happened here?"

"Yes. Pierre's been arrested."

"Pierre arrested! What on earth for?"

"Well, they're trying to make out he killed old Février. There were four cops searched the *Centaur* this morning when she came in. They've taken him to jail in Rouen."

"The hell they have!"

Charles beckoned to Babette; he wanted to say a few words to her and then leave.

As she went past him, tray in hand, she said in a low voice: "I've something to tell you. Don't go."

Everyone knew that Charles was in the café listening to what was said. Nonetheless, they went on airing their views about his brother, and his family, too, without raising their voices.

"Think he did it?"

"Well, seeing as his poor mother was always harping on it, saying she wanted it to happen—it makes one think, don't it?"

Paumelle called Babette and made a point of holding her in talk. Charles was beginning to regret this visit to the Amiral and to wish he'd kept to his first idea of going home and staying with his mother for a while. He made a last attempt.

"Babette!"

"Just a moment."

But then her employer sent her down to the cellar for some gin, and Paumelle looked across at Charles and grinned offensively.

Charles's attachment had lasted for a year, and he spent almost all his spare time at the Amiral—to the point of making himself ridiculous. Yet he'd have found it hard to say what it was about Babette that attracted him so much. She was far from a beauty, hardly even pretty. Thin, pale-faced, with eyes of an indeterminate color— "dishwater eyes," Pierre used to call them laughingly— her hair always uncombed, she had little to recommend her but the grace of youth. And she lacked animation; you could never tell if she was pleased or sad; "as if she didn't give a damn for anything or anyone," as Pierre had once remarked of her.

What Charles got out of it came to very little. A kiss or two snatched behind the kitchen door in an odor of fried herring; a hurried embrace on the sidewalk outside when dusk was falling—and even then she pressed herself against him with more docility than passion.

Nevertheless, he'd have been capable of killing Paumelle, or anyone else for that matter, who got between him and Babette! He had to face the disapproval of his family; of his aunt Lachaume in particular, who had always wanted him to marry her daughter, Berthe, the girl he had met going home from church.

"Babette!" His voice was rough with anger. "If you speak another word to Paumelle . . ."

"Ssh! Come outside for a moment."

Some of the men in the café exchanged amused glances

when they saw this man of thirty-three meekly following the girl outside, like a boy of sixteen in the throes of his first love affair.

"Well? What is it?"

They were standing in the rain, near the tide gate, and Babette's red-gold curls were blown back by the sea wind.

"I've only just remembered. This morning, when I saw that superintendent . . ."

"Yes?"

He was still in a bad humor; the thought that Paumelle was still in the café, to which Babette would be returning in a moment, haunted his mind.

"I remember now that he came here last week, that superintendent, and he stopped in at the Amiral. It was two days after the *Centaur* sailed. He asked me if your brother would be at sea for long, and I told him that depended on the catch."

"Did he ask you any other questions?"

"Only one. He wanted to know if Pierre had got his letter all right."

"What letter?"

"The one that came for him on the second, the day the *Centaur* got back. She left again next morning, of course."

"Oh? Pierre got a letter, did he? Where did it come from?"

"I don't know. I think it had a French stamp. If it had been a foreign one, I'd have noticed."

"And the superintendent asked you about it?"

He was wondering what it meant. True, the Café de l'Amiral was used as a mail address by a good many fishermen, especially those who lived outside town and found it more convenient to get their letters at Jules's. But this was not a practice of Pierre's. And, still stranger, Pierre hadn't breathed a word to him about this letter.

"Well, I'll have to be getting back." The wind was cold, and Babette's teeth were chattering. "What are you going to do?"

"I'm going to Rouen."

"Kiss me . . . Hurry up!"

But just then the door of the café opened; Jules poked his head out and shouted to Babette to come at once.

"Too bad. I'll catch the train at five past midnight."

And, though conscious that he was making himself ridiculous, he followed her back to the café. After ordering a glass of rum, he fell to pondering deeply, knitting his brows.

This business of the letter was disquieting. Why, for one thing, hadn't Pierre shown it to him? That alone was more than strange—unprecedented. It was common knowledge that, where letters were concerned, Pierre simply washed his hands of them. "Show it to Charles," he would say. "I can't be bothered." Or, "I'll sign if Charles tells me to."

Indeed, it was Charles, with his methodical mind and tireless industry, who was the brains of the combination. So much so, that when Pierre was studying for his master mariner's license, Charles had to spend laborious days studying the manuals and expounding them to his twin brother.

Obviously there might be some quite simple explanation of that letter. For instance, Pierre might be having an affair with a girl. No, it could hardly be that. On the rare occasions when Pierre had wanted to compose a love letter, he had always asked his brother to help him out. . . . Now what exactly had happened on that day, February second? Why hadn't Charles come to the Amiral at the usual hour? He racked his brain to remember, and wished he had a sheet of paper on which to jot down his recollections one by one. It always helped him to think clearly, having the facts before him in black and white.

Ah, yes, that was it. He'd promised his mother to stay home for dinner. So when the *Centaur* reached port, he was still at the dinner table. What happened next? He called Babette.

"What time exactly did you hand him that letter?"

"When he came here . . . Almost immediately."

So, on coming ashore, Pierre had gone to the Amiral for the traditional glass of laced coffee.

What had happened after that? . . . Charles was surprised to find how difficult it was to get a clear idea of one's movements of only ten days before. One thing was certain: he, Charles, had gone to the Amiral, since he never missed an evening there. Probably he'd come at about eight, soon after dinner.

Yes! Now it came back to him. He'd asked about his brother, and was told he'd gone back to the *Centaur* with the blacksmith; there had been some small repair to make. Then he, Charles, had gone down to the dock and found Pierre standing on the slippery iron deck watching the unloading.

Had there been anything unusual in Pierre's manner? Had he looked worried, for instance? In spite of himself, Charles had begun scribbling on the marble top of the table.

No. Pierre had had the rather preoccupied expression of a skipper whose boat is due to sail in a few hours' time and who has to keep track of what's being done on board his ship meanwhile; no more than that.

He had certainly asked Charles: "How's Mother today?"

And Charles had replied: "Much the same."

This wasn't quite accurate. She'd had another "attack," and its cause had been the usual one: an encounter with Monsieur Février in the street. All her attacks followed similar lines, varying only in their intensity. Monsieur Février would see her coming toward him, unmindful of everything else, of the people around her, the policeman on duty; then, in a low, clear voice, her eyes fastened on him, she would launch into one of her denunciations, couched in semi-Biblical phraseology.

"Mark my words, evil man! Three of them have gone to their deaths, and my dear husband, Pierre, is waiting for the fourth to join them and the Lord's will to be accomplished. Can you not feel the end is near? Do you not know your presence here on earth is an abomination?"

A gaunt, menacing figure, all in black, with fever-bright eyes, she dogged his steps. A crowd quickly gathered, and it was a painful spectacle. The old man's attempts to shake her off by turning into shops were unavailing, and he did not dare say anything to Madame Canut for fear of making things worse.

Charles was quite certain that on February second he hadn't told his brother about his mother's attack. As usual, he had kept to the subject of Babette and his scruples about marrying her; there was no knowing how his mother would take it, having a daughter-in-law in the house.

For Charles was made that way; he was almost morbidly afraid of causing distress or hurting anyone's feelings. He was always making apologies—even when someone else stepped on his toes.

He had spent the rest of that evening in the usual way; had gone to the Amiral and seated himself near the bar. After finishing his work on the *Centaur*, Pierre had entered the café with some friends.

"You'll be coming home tonight to sleep?" Charles had asked him.

That, as far as he could remember, had been the course of events. He, Charles, had gone home by himself, since his brother showed no inclination to make a move. And presumably Pierre had stayed out late, because he had not heard him enter the house. Then, at seven the next morning, the *Centaur* had sailed.

It was at eight that Monsieur Février's cleaning woman, Tatine, had found her employer lying dead on the floor of his living room.

But what about that letter? Charles's face was flushed with the strain of trying to unravel its significance. Moreover, how could the superintendent have known that his brother had received a letter, on that precise day, at the Amiral?

"Babette! Think hard! Are you sure he didn't say anything else to you, that policeman?"

Just then he noticed Paumelle eying him with an offensive leer, and very nearly flung his glass in the young man's face.

"There's another thing," he continued. "It's terribly important. What time did my brother leave the café that evening?"

"I'm afraid I didn't notice. But I remember that we closed quite early—about midnight, I think."

He had to let it go at that. It was high time to be starting for his train. And that swine Paumelle would stay on here with Babette! And, now that he remembered it, he hadn't kissed her once this evening. Still, all that could wait. The big thing was to have a talk with Pierre, if only for a few moments; surely they couldn't refuse him that? And to have a word with the examining magistrate as well, if that was possible. . . .

He began his journey in the badly lighted little local train, which, as usual, was almost empty; there were only three other passengers. It connected with the main line at La Bréauté. The express came in with a rattle and a roar, brightly lighted from end to end, and Charles jumped into a compartment full of soldiers and sailors on leave. At Rouen he impatiently shook off the shadowy forms that emerged from the darkness and tried to take his arm as he made his way to a hotel he knew, near the market. He gave instructions to be called at seven o'clock.

He had a bad night—but that was only to be expected, anyhow. His good nights were rare. In the daytime, it was all right; his work kept his mind busy, and when he thought at all, it was usually of Babette. But once he was lying in the darkness, a curious, subtle warmth began to permeate his body. He knew it was fever, and also knew what that fever meant.

26

"You should get a transfer to some place at a high altitude," the doctor had advised him six years earlier. "The Fécamp climate doesn't suit you."

But what about his mother? And his brother? And Babette? How would they manage without him, or he without them? For Charles was like that: he needed to feel indispensable to others and others indispensable to him. He couldn't live without affection, and warm affection at that. He enjoyed hearing people say—and his friends often said it in his hearing, to please him: "Those Canut brothers are inseparable, like Siamese twins. One couldn't live without the other." And he smiled happily when someone added, "They're the perfect team. Pierre has the brawn and Charles supplies the brains."

But at night there was no question of his smiling; he felt so wretchedly alone and ill. Sometimes he could hardly breathe; he seemed to be slowly suffocating. It was unfair, he thought, that this should have happened to him, of all people, considering that he had never done anyone any harm, but, on the contrary, had always helped others in their troubles. Once his thoughts had taken this course, he always wound up by picturing his funeral, the mourners following in black, with his brother heading the procession, his eyes red and puffy.

At last he managed to doze off, woke a few minutes before seven, and hurried down to the restaurant. A group of market gardeners, who had just come in from the country with their produce, were breakfasting in the middle of the room. A morning paper lay on one of the tables, and a word, its last letter hidden by a fold, caught his eye: "murderer."

With a casual air, he picked up the paper and settled down in a corner to read the article. It was in the middle of the front page, with a headline splashed over three columns.

GRIM SAGA OF THE SEA RECALLED

Then, in smaller type: *"Arrest of Pierre Canut, alleged murderer of M. Emile Février. Sensational developments expected."*

He almost called "Babette!" The mere fact of being in a café made him feel she must be near. But the waitress here was a fat, phlegmatic peasant girl, who had deposited her clogs at the kitchen door and was shuffling about in slippers.

The arrest of Pierre Canut, captain of the *Centaur*, a Fécamp trawler, which took place early this morning, has provoked much excitement among the local fishermen. The murder of M. Février ten days ago would seem to be the aftermath of some remarkable happenings on the high seas off Rio de Janeiro in the year 1906.

The following account of what may rank as one of the strangest sagas of the sea is compiled from stories in the papers of that period, when sailing ships were still in general use. At that time Fécamp was the home port not only of Newfoundland "bankers"—of which some still survive—but of a four-master, the *Télémaque*, commanded by Captain Rolland, plying between France and Chile.

In the winter of 1906 the news reached France that the *Télémaque* had gone down, with all hands, off Rio de Janeiro. But exactly four weeks later, an English tramp steamer on her way to Cape Horn sighted a ship's boat in which were five men, dead or dying of starvation.

Four of them slowly recovered. The fifth, who had a curious gash on his wrist, was already dead when taken on board the tramp.

The four survivors were: Emile Février, aged 36, of Fécamp, boatswain; Martin Paumelle, aged 20, able seaman, of Les Loges; Jacques Berniquet, aged 26, topman, of Bénouville; Antoine Le Flem, aged 36, ship's carpenter, of Paimpol.

The dead man was Pierre Canut, aged 24, of Fécamp.

Harrowing revelations were made in the course of the official inquiry that followed. It was learned that, in the beginning, there were six survivors in the boat, the sixth being a British sailor, Roger Paterson of Plymouth, aged 45.

They ran out of food first, then water. And Paterson, who was less robust than the others, died.

We have before us the statements made by the survivors. Some portions are of too ghastly a nature to make public in our columns. We must remember that these men had been adrift in an open boat for a fortnight and had become so weak that they could hardly speak or move. It was on the fourteenth day after Paterson's death that Février, who had been on voyages in the Arctic seas, set the example by slitting a vein in Paterson's wrist while the body was still warm.

After the Englishman's body was thrown overboard, drained of its last drop of blood, the five men had a brief return of strength, but it lasted only a couple of days; then they relapsed into a state of semidelirious exhaustion.

The authorities, not without good reason, put searching questions as to the origin of the wound on Canut's wrist. The four survivors were examined separately and at great length, at a time when their physical condition was such that, we may assume, they lacked the capacity to falsify the facts; and no pains were spared to elicit the truth.

Their statements were all to the same effect and, under the circumstances, may be accepted as substantially correct. According to these statements, Canut cut his own wrist with his knife in a sudden access of delirium, on the very day they were rescued.

Canut was a married man. He left a widow, whom he had married only some eight months previously and who, at the time of his death, was expected to give birth to twins in the near future.

While reading, Charles had gulped down a large mug of coffee, hardly conscious that he was doing so, and now he felt slightly sick. He gazed with unseeing eyes at the people in the restaurant, who were eating heartily and talking at the top of their voices. This experience of reading in a newspaper about things that were so familiar to him had had a curious effect. On the printed page they seemed to have undergone some subtle change. It was like the impression one sometimes has when revisiting a place where one has lived as a child—nothing is quite as one remembers it.

Also it surprised him that they had been able to compress the whole tragic narrative into a few brief paragraphs. The journalist went on to talk of the survivors and their subsequent lives. "We have been unable to ascertain what became of Berniquet and Le Flem."

Charles could have told him. How could he have failed to know, considering how closely these men's lives became linked with his own and those of his family?

After being lost sight of for ten years, Martin Paumelle had returned to Fécamp, bought an old cutter, *La Fran-çoise,* and earned a scant livelihood by inshore fishing. He had taken to drinking, was rarely sober, and the only man he had been able to get to work for him was an unfortunate young fellow known locally as "the Twister," who was subject to epileptic fits.

All sorts of stories had circulated about the curious pair, the drunkard and the epileptic; their hairbreadth escapes were proverbial, and the Fécamp lifeboat had had to go out to their rescue oftener than for all the other fishermen put together. Drink had the effect of making Paumelle lachrymose, and he was always buttonholing people, bewailing his hard luck, cadging drinks—with the result that the innkeepers did their best to keep him out of their premises. A local prostitute, with whom he lived for a time, had presented him with a son, after which she had gone away, leaving the child in Paumelle's hands.

Paumelle Senior had come to a gruesome end at the age of fifty-three, crushed literally to a jelly between the hull of his cutter and the dock. His memory survived in the person of his son, the young man who called Babette "dear" and was Charles's *bête noire*.

As for Le Flem, he had migrated to West Africa and evidently made money, because later on he returned to France and set himself up as a building contractor in Niort, where he married a girl who came of a good family. He had died in his bed of some internal disease, at the age of sixty-five, leaving a daughter, Adèle, whose age, Charles judged, must now be about twenty. This accounted for the second survivor.

Berniquet, the other man referred to by the journalist, had kept to a seafaring life, become a skipper-owner of a tug at Ostend, and never returned to his hometown. Or, rather, he had returned once only, for a brief visit, when his mother died.

On the night after the funeral, which took place at Bénouville, he had started back on foot along the cliff road to Etretat. Unaware that, owing to landslides, the configuration of the cliff had changed since his boyhood, he had fallen to his death from a height of more than three hundred feet.

Then the only one remaining was Février. The newspaper had this to say about him.

M. Février did not return to Europe. After the inquiry he settled down at Guayaquil, where he joined a ship plying between Ecuador and the Galápagos; after that, a French Line freighter serving the coasts of Chile and Peru.

At Guayaquil he made the acquaintance of a Frenchwoman from Fécamp, Georgette Robin, who was employed as a maid in a Chilean household, and married her. After some years, however, they separated.

Then an uncle at Fécamp died, leaving him his house, Villa des Mouettes, and ten years ago M. Février returned to France and settled down there. By all accounts M. Février had developed into an inoffensive, rather shy old man, who kept to himself as much as possible and rarely visited the town. One of the reasons why he refrained from appearing in the streets was the possibility of encountering Mme Canut, the widow of the dead seaman. . . .

Charles guessed what was coming, and couldn't bring himself to read it. Really, they had no business publishing such things in the papers. Those women, for instance, selling cauliflower and celery in the doorway—what business was it of theirs that his mother was . . .

Of course she was "mental," as they say; but she was far from being insane in the ordinary sense. Her madness was of a special, restricted kind; that, indeed, was why there had never been any reason to send her to an asylum.

In matters of daily life she behaved like ordinary women; in fact, she kept her house exceptionally well and was a skillful cook. Now and again, once or twice a day, her sister, who kept the pastry shop three doors up the street, would drop in to see that all was well; that was all. Nevertheless, she would have fits of weeping and talking to herself, which could last a whole afternoon. And there were days when, without any warning and at the most inappropriate moment—when, for example, she was at the creamery, buying butter—she would break into one of her rambling monologues:

"I'd have you know, my friends, that there are only two of them left now. The mills of God grind slowly, but the end is certain. A day will come when all of them are dead, and my husband's soul can rest in peace."

For she kept track of all those men who, she firmly believed, had done to her husband what they had done to the English sailor. She was indefatigable in collecting information, and had been the first to know of Le Flem's death.

In the beginning, her attacks had been few and far between; it was only after Février's coming to live in

Fécamp that they grew more frequent. His presence was a constant reminder of her loss, and she was convinced that not till he had died could her dead husband's soul "be at peace."

Charles called the waitress. "Give me a small brandy." Brandy never agreed with him, but he needed something strong this morning. The thought of all those columns in the papers, the knowledge that for a paltry sum anyone could pry into the intimate details of his mother's life, made him hot with shame.

As though the article on the front page were not enough, "they" had another on the third, under the headline TRIUMPH OF DETECTION.

From the technical point of view, the investigation of this case, as conducted by M. Laroche, the examining magistrate, and Superintendent Gentil, ranks as a model of the manner in which such inquiries should be conducted.

On arriving at the villa at 8:00 A.M. on February 3, M. Février's cleaning woman, a local character known to everyone as "Tatine," was surprised to see light showing through a crack in the curtains of the living-room window. She assumed that her employer had forgotten to turn off the lights when going up to bed.

We can picture her horror when, on opening the living-room door, she saw the old man lying with his throat cut, in a pool of blood.

Rushing to the front door, she screamed for help, and some neighbors were quickly on the scene. The police were sent for, and it is satisfactory to learn that the first people on the scene of the crime had, for once, had the sense to leave things exactly as they found them.

At two o'clock M. Laroche, Superintendent Gentil, and a detective inspector arrived at Fécamp, and the investigation began. Our local police are nothing if not thorough, and we can be sure that nothing escaped our superintendent's eagle eye. Two glasses standing on the table, one half full of gin, showed that not long before his death M. Février had had a visitor with whom he was acquainted and of whom he had no suspicions.

There was another valuable clue. The knife used by the murderer was lying in the pool of blood. A jackknife with a lanyard of the kind sailors use, it had evidently seen long service, and bore, roughly engraved on the handle, the initials P. C.

M. Février's house was kept in excellent order and the floors were highly polished, a fact that did not fail to attract the attention of the police, who at once made a search for footprints in the living room and hall.

The police doctor fixed the time of the murder as about midnight, and we may assume that, shortly before that hour, M. Février had a visitor. Contrary to his practice (he usually retired at nine or ten o'clock) he was still up, and he went to open the front door.

It was raining hard that night, and the caller, who was wearing clogs, took them off and left them just outside the living-room door. He evidently had slippers on under the clogs, for traces of damp slippers could be clearly seen on the polished floor.

It is to be presumed that a quarrel ensued. There were lines of footprints up and down the room, suggesting that the man had paced it in a state of extreme agitation. After that he evidently sat down for a while; on examining one of the chairs, the superintendent made an important discovery: some herring scales were sticking to the cushion.

These facts go far to prove that M. Février's assailant was a sailor, and a sailor who had come straight to the villa from his ship. And the only ship that came in at Fécamp that evening was the *Centaur*.

In view of the fact that the deceased had evidently been expecting this visit, his cleaning woman was questioned closely on this point. From her statement it appears that two days previously her employer, having been accosted in the street, as frequently happened, by Mme Canut, had written a letter, which he had given to her to mail. The letter was for Captain Pierre Canut, and addressed, "Café de l'Amiral, Fécamp."

The strictest secrecy was called for in this inquiry, and we must commend the discretion of all concerned. Like most Fécamp trawlers, the *Centaur* is equipped with a radio, and at the time, Canut was at sea within easy reach of the British coast. Also we must not forget that Canut's twin brother lives at Fécamp and is intensely devoted to his skipper brother.

The police decline to enlighten us as to the manner in which they procured a pair of clogs owned by Captain Canut. All we can say is that the prints made by these corresponded exactly with those found in the hall of M. Février's house.

Superintendent Gentil has ascertained that, soon after landing, on the evening of the second, Canut received the letter sent to him by the deceased.

Thus, while there was ample evidence to justify an arrest, extreme secrecy was essential; otherwise the murderer might have landed somewhere on the English coast.

Actually, even Canut's brother, Charles, had not the least suspicion of what was impending, and the police had no difficulty in effecting Canut's arrest as soon as the *Centaur* reached Fécamp. The prisoner gave no resistance, though there were some protestations from his crew and the local people.

We are informed that, after at first denying that he had visited the Villa des Mouettes on the night of the crime, he has finally admitted that he went there. This, in our opinion, may prove to be the first step toward a full confession of the crime.

# 3

NOBODY'D HAVE thought it of Pierre Canut, to look at him. Yet the mildest rebuke from Monsieur Pessart, who always spoke in moderate terms and never raised his voice, was enough to set the burly skipper blushing like a schoolboy called to order. And in his early days, when studying for examinations, he had constantly lost confidence in himself.

"It's no use, Charles; I'll never be able to learn all that stuff. And, anyhow, luck's always been against us. They'll fail me, for sure."

Charles would then tell him not to talk nonsense; he'd coach him. And a moment later Pierre would be laughing at his fears. All the same, it showed that Pierre was far from being as sure of himself as his tough appearance would lead one to believe.

That was why, as the hours dragged on, Charles's anxiety steadily increased; heaven alone knew what Pierre might say or do now that "they" had him in their clutches.

"I can't tell you. Try that fellow at the end of the corridor, on the left."

Charles went there and politely raised his cap to a

haughty attendant, who didn't even trouble to hear him out.

"This is the Commercial Court. What you want is the examining magistrate's office."

He had come to the Law Courts at an early hour, when the corridors were practically empty. Now the flagstones were thickly smeared with traces of muddy shoes; lawyers in flapping gowns were pacing up and down, stopping to exchange a jest or a greeting, and other people—people like Canut—were scanning the notices posted on the doors, then moving on despondently. Charles went up to a man who appeared to be on duty outside one of the offices.

"Could you tell me where to find the examining magistrate? His name is Monsieur Laroche, I believe."

The man turned to a policeman beside him. "Know if he's coming in this morning?"

"Maybe, but I doubt it."

"It's most important," Charles said, "and I'd be very grateful if you'd tell me. I'm the brother of Captain Canut, who was arrested yesterday at Fécamp. That's why I've got to see him."

"See who? Your brother?"

It amazed him that these men, who probably had had troubles of their own and knew what it meant to be up against it, men who were, after all, so much like himself, should show so little fellow feeling and grudge even a minute, less than a minute, of their time to help him out. After some moments' silence, rather reluctantly, it seemed, the policeman deigned to add some words of explanation.

"I don't think you'll be allowed to see him at this stage of the case. Still, you can always try. There's just a chance the magistrate will turn up today, and you can tackle him."

Whereupon the two men turned their backs and resumed the conversation he had interrupted—about private affairs of a not too savory order—and paid no more heed to Charles, who spent the next two and a half hours on a wooden bench, musing disconsolately on the unfairness of it all.

The first thing, obviously, was to convince the magistrate that he absolutely must see his brother. Otherwise Pierre would give way to despondency, abandon hope, and make no effort to stand up to "them." He, Charles, would go straight to the point.

"Did you do it, Pierre?"

And Pierre's answer would settle it; then he'd know where he stood. Not that this was really necessary: it couldn't possibly have been Pierre. For one thing, if Pierre had killed old Février, he would not have used a knife, or done it in that way, by slitting his victim's throat. Nor would he have stolen anything; not by the wildest stretch of imagination could one see Pierre as a thief.

All that would need explaining to the magistrate, and Pierre was quite incapable of it. Charles could picture him mumbling ineffective answers, staring at the floor, and dimly wondering what all the fuss was about.

Four o'clock struck. Half past four.

"Do you really think he'll be coming?"

One of the men at the door had settled down to reading official-looking documents, while the policeman, his hands clasped behind his back, stared down at the courtyard.

"Hold on! There's the police wagon. Perhaps he's in it."

No; when the van drew up in a corner of the yard, no one got out of it, and the driver went across the street to have a drink.

Charles hadn't foreseen anything of this sort when, at Fécamp, he decided to go to Rouen to see his brother. Even the look of the building in which he now sat was a surprise. In some ways it recalled the military hospital in which, owing to someone's forgetfulness, he had been kept waiting for two hours, bare to the waist, in a drafty corridor rather like this one.

"What are you doing here?" someone had finally asked him. "Get dressed and get out."

He didn't dare rise and pace the muddy flagstones; he was straining his ears to catch every sound, and now and again he gave a start and gazed eagerly down the corridor. But usually it was only a clerk carrying a bundle of documents from one office to another.

On these occasions the man to whom Charles had spoken first, seeing him about to rise, shook his head to indicate that it wasn't Monsieur Laroche. Sometimes an electric bell purred at the end of the corridor and a disk with a number on it appeared on a board. A dapper, self-important little man walked by, and the men on duty rose and said respectfully, "Good morning, sir." From a remark made to the policeman, Charles gathered that the man who had gone by was the public prosecutor.

But why couldn't these people come to work at fixed hours, like everybody else; why were they so elusive? Talking and laughing, two men came down the corridor, and when they reached an office door, stood aside mock ceremonially, each saying "After you" and smiling. The clerk beckoned to Charles.

"That was he. Now, if you'll fill out this form . . ."

"What's it for?"

"Just write your name and why you want to see him."

Charles did so. After his name, he wrote: "I have some important things to tell you about my brother"—adding, after a moment's thought—"who is innocent of the crime."

He followed the clerk to the door of the office. When it opened, he heard the magistrate and his friend talking, then a voice asking: "What is it?"

The door had remained open, and Charles heard the same voice saying in a low tone: "It's the brother of the fellow I was telling you about. He wants to have an interview."

"Yes? Will you see him?"

How maddening to hear all this and be unable to put in

a word; to know how easy it could be, that there were only a few steps to take, a threshold to cross—and it was forbidden him to cross it!

"Tell him I'll notify him if and when I wish to hear his statement."

Charles saw the clerk return, not in the least embarrassed by having to transmit this message. Indeed, his tone was quite casual when he repeated it to Charles, word for word. After a moment he asked: "Well? What are you waiting for?"

For nothing, evidently! He was only thinking—thinking of the bad luck that dogged him and his family at every turn, and of the unfairness of it all. Even in their own street at Fécamp there were people—people who didn't *think*—who would refer to "the Canuts" in the same tone as they might speak of "the Lachaumes" or "the Bertrands." They had no notion of what it meant to be a Canut; to have begun life in the situation in which he and Pierre were born; to have had a mother who was half the time in tears and talked to herself for hours on end, in tones that made your flesh creep.

True, her sister, Madame Lachaume, whom the children called "Aunt Lou," came now and again to cast an eye on things. But she was only an aunt, after all, and they could never feel really at home when she had them spend the day with her, at the spotlessly white shop, in a sickly sweet odor of hot cakes and pastry.

Then, after a particularly severe "attack," there would be one of those family gatherings at which it was discussed whether or not their mother should be shut up.

Even at school they were apt to be reminded of the family tragedy, when one of the boys would ask, goggling his eyes: "Hey, Canut, is it true that your father was eaten by his shipmates?"

Worst of all, so odious that they hardly dared to think of them, were the occasions when, as boys, they had been sent to beg for some money, just enough to pay the rent, from the owner of the *Télémaque*.

It had poisoned all their childhood, his and Pierre's— the feeling that they were a family apart, unlike others. . . .

As Charles was walking down the big central corridor of the Law Courts, he stopped abruptly and seemed to wake up from a dream. From an elaborately carved doorway on his left came the sound of a man speaking in a strident, emphatic voice. A lawyer was addressing the court. Glancing in, he saw some other lawyers in black gowns seated on a bench beside the door, like ordinary litigants waiting their turn. His gaze settled on one of them, a small, plump, rosy-cheeked man, far more like a peasant than a lawyer—even his gown, as he wore it, brought to mind a peasant smock. He looked so good-natured that Charles decided to risk it, and, politely taking off his cap, went up to him.

"Excuse me, sir . . ."

"Put on your cap. Have you been summoned to appear?"

"No. It's about my brother."

It embarrassed him to have to talk like this, in public; the other men on the bench were staring at him, listening. He'd have preferred to call the red-cheeked man aside, but did not dare propose it. Though the morning papers had devoted several columns to the "Fécamp Murder," the lawyer seemed puzzled when Charles mentioned his brother's name, and turned to a colleague with an inquiring look. The other man nodded; he, evidently, knew about it.

"A counsel for the defense has been appointed by the court."

"Who?"

"That young fellow Abeille, I was told."

"You hear that? A lawyer has been appointed, our friend Maître Abeille."

"Could you tell me where to find him?"

The lawyers exchanged glances again.

"Isn't he appearing in Small Claims Court?"

"No. I wouldn't be surprised but what he's gone to Fécamp." The man turned to Charles. "The best thing you can do is look him up in the telephone directory and give him a call."

Then he went back to talking with his friends. Their interest, such as it was, in Charles's troubles had evaporated. For half an hour he roamed the Law Courts looking for Abeille, not without a secret hope that by some happy fluke he might run into the examining magistrate somewhere in the building.

Though he was sparing no effort to come to his brother's aid, he was haunted by a sense of guilt. Probably, he decided, this was because he had spent the previous evening at the Amiral, to be with Babette; and also because he'd left home without saying good-bye to his mother.

In a café, he called up Abeille. A servant informed him he was out, and she couldn't say when he'd be back.

"But I expect," she added, "he'll be here for dinner, though I can't say positively. Anyhow, if you call here tomorrow morning at about ten, you're sure to find him."

Was there anything else he should try? He would have to get back to Fécamp before midnight, to arrange things with Filloux about substituting for him at the station.

He returned to his hotel, which was more a tavern than an inn, and was patronized chiefly by small farmers of the neighborhood. Wicker cages containing fowl had been dumped in the taproom, and Charles ate to the accompaniment of their cackling. For the evening meal the waitress, after cleaning her hands with a scouring brush, had donned a moderately clean apron. On the table at which he was eating, a square of brown oilcloth did duty for a tablecloth.

It was nothing new for Charles to stay for hours quietly

seated at a café table, but tonight his nerves were stretched, and several times he felt like jumping up and letting out a volley of curses. Every thought that crossed his mind was odious—not least the thought that at this moment Babette was serving drinks to customers at the Amiral and some of them might be taking liberties with her.

Aunt Lou or Berthe was with his mother, he supposed. Perhaps they had persuaded her to stay the night at their place, where there was a bedroom free now that Aunt Lou's son was with his regiment in the Alps.

But what about Pierre?

"No!" he suddenly exclaimed, rising from his chair. No! It was unthinkable that Pierre should spend the night in custody. He absolutely *must* do something, and without a moment's delay.

He called up the lawyer, and this time a man's voice answered.

"Maître Abeille speaking. What do you want?"

"I'm Charles Canut, Pierre Canut's brother. I'm in Rouen, and I'd like to see you."

"When?"

"Immediately, if possible. Pierre is innocent, and . . ."

He could hear the man at the other end in conversation with someone. Then the lawyer said: "Listen! Couldn't you possibly come tomorrow morning instead?"

"No. I must see you now."

"Very well, then. But I can give you only a few minutes."

Better than nothing! Already Charles felt a vast relief. He went, almost at a run, to the lawyer's home, which was on the third floor of a big apartment house near the docks. An elevator took him up; the door was opened by the maid who had answered his first telephone call. She gave him a long, interested scrutiny.

"So you're Charles Canut? Will you wait a minute, please?"

Leaving him in the hall, she opened a door at the far end. A sound of laughter, the chink of glasses, whiffs of cigar smoke came through the doorway; evidently a party was in progress.

"Show him into my study. Tell him I won't be long."

To these people it meant nothing, of course; Abeille wouldn't dream of breaking off a conversation just begun because his client's brother had some communication to impart. As he waited, cap in hand, Charles brooded on the callousness of Abeille and his kind; was it that they didn't understand or simply didn't care? Then he heard a young, cheerful voice behind him.

"You must excuse me if I can give you only a few minutes. We are having a little party here tonight."

The two men stared at each other, both somewhat surprised. Charles was taken aback no less by the youth of the man who had addressed him—he seemed to be in his middle twenties—than by his general appearance; he looked less like a lawyer than a professional dancer. And Abeille hadn't expected to see a mild, painfully shy young fellow in a railwayman's uniform.

"Sit down, won't you? Unfortunately, I haven't got my brief yet, so I really know nothing about the case except what I've read in the papers. However, I shall be seeing the magistrate and your brother tomorrow—and then we will know where we stand."

Charles found nothing to answer. The lawyer lit his cigar, which had gone out, and held a cigarette case toward his visitor.

"No, thanks. I don't smoke."

"I gather you have something to tell me. What is it?"

"It's this. My brother is innocent."

The lawyer shrugged his shoulders, as if to convey: "Naturally! You were bound to say that." Aloud he said: "Has he an alibi?"

"I couldn't say. That's one of the reasons why I've got to see him. It's hard to explain, but Pierre is so used to having me look after his affairs, except his fishing of course, that . . ."

From the room at the end of the hall came a woman's laugh.

"Yes, yes. But what exactly do you want?"

"I want to see my brother."

"Well, you may have to wait a bit. I can't say anything definite, but, judging by the way the investigation is being carried on, I doubt if Laroche will let you see him. Not, in any case, before he's got a confession."

"A confession! But, as I told you, my brother didn't do it."

"Quite so. Quite so . . . Well, the best thing you can do is give me your address in Rouen. You'll be staying here some days, won't you? I'll go into the matter tomorrow. The moment I have some news for you, I'll let you know."

The lawyer was standing, haloed with blue cigar smoke, and smiling amiably.

"And now, I'm afraid I must ask you to excuse me. My guests . . ."

For some time Charles had had a look of frowning concentration and been swaying slightly—sure signs with a Norman that he is pondering some drastic step and how to take it. After a moment's silence, he asked quite calmly: "I suppose there's nothing to prevent my engaging another lawyer, is there?"

Abeille very nearly let his cigar drop. His lips were quivering. To gain time, he muttered: "Eh? What did you say?"

"I said that, since I'm paying, I've the right to choose the lawyer I think best."

"Try, by all means, if you feel like that." Abeille showed his teeth in a rather sickly grin as he moved toward the door. "Yes, I heartily advise you to try—think of the excellent effect it would have on the court! Not to mention that you may find it somewhat difficult to persuade any of my colleagues to take the case from me. . . . Good evening,

Monsieur Canut. This way. The door on the right. Yes, that's it."

He slammed the door behind Charles, who, indignant but secretly somewhat relieved, walked slowly down the three flights of stairs.

Was it done deliberately or merely due to chance? In any case, Pierre had been left all day in his cell and had seen nobody except his jailer. And, after a night's uneasy sleep, he had to wait till ten in the morning before the door opened and a gruff voice said: "You're wanted. Come!"

He hadn't shaved or even thought of washing. And he was still in his sea clothes: a woolen shirt, a flannel undershirt, a thick sweater, and cold, stiff oilskins, which hampered his movements.

"Get in."

He hardly noticed that the vehicle was a police van. In the dark interior he felt a series of jolts from roughly cobbled streets and heard familiar sounds: cries of street hawkers, strident voices of housewives at their marketing, a church bell ringing, car horns, a dog barking—the noise and bustle of a big town going about its morning business.

When the door of the van opened and he got out, he blinked at a sunbeam slanting across the quadrangle of the Law Courts—so bright and slender that it brought to mind the golden rays one sees in missals lighting up saints' faces.

Before he had taken a dozen steps, a group formed around him; press photographers clicked their cameras, then backed hastily for full-length shots.

He didn't flinch, but it seemed as if, handcuffed though he was, he had half a mind to lash out at them or shoo them away like pestering insects.

He was led up flights of stairs, through a maze of passages, and finally made to sit on a bench between two policemen. A quarter of an hour later, a young lawyer, his gown flapping as he hurried past, entered a nearby office.

Five minutes passed; then the door of the office opened and Canut was let in.

"Sit down," said Monsieur Laroche in a toneless voice. "This is Maître Abeille, the counsel officially appointed for your defense."

Canut gazed at Abeille, who was drawing a sheaf of papers from his briefcase with a self-important air. Then he glanced briefly at the examining magistrate's clerk, who struck him as the most human-looking of the three.

"Now I shall put a few questions to you, and I must ask you to weigh your answers well. If you wish, you may consult your lawyer before replying."

The words fell on his ears like hollow sounds without significance. Only with an effort and by repeating the sounds to himself did he grasp their meaning. And all the time his thoughts kept wandering off. Just now, for instance, he was thinking: He's the same sort of man as Monsieur Pessart, I would say. He couldn't have explained what the magistrate had in common with Monsieur Pessart; but for some reason the idea fixed itself in his mind.

"My first question is of a rather delicate nature, but I am obliged to put it. Is it a fact that, rightly or wrongly, your mother held Monsieur Février responsible for her husband's death?"

Canut sighed. He had a feeling that the whole business was going to be absurdly complicated. Yet how simple it might have been! They had only to ask him a few plain, straightforward questions.

"Answer me, please."

"There's no answer needed; it's a matter of common knowledge."

"Very good." He turned to his clerk. "Write down that the prisoner admits this fact. . . . My next question is: Was not your mother's hostility to the deceased based on a particularly revolting allegation—a charge of cannibalism, to put it bluntly?"

The lawyer shuffled and cleared his throat, to remind them of his presence. But Canut had already answered wearily: "Yes . . . What next?"

The magistrate turned again to the clerk. "Get that down, please. The prisoner also admits the fact stated in my second question." After examining the papers in the file, he selected one and continued: "I find in this report that, subsequent to Monsieur Février's return to Fécamp, there were frequent public altercations between him and your mother, though he did his best to keep out of her way."

Canut had a twisted smile. "My poor mother—well, she's not quite all there."

"Now, pay attention to this. Two months ago your brother wrote a letter to the deceased. It was found in his desk by the police, and I have it here."

Canut looked up quickly; this was the first he had heard of this letter.

"Perhaps I need not read it out to you in full," the magistrate continued, "since it covers several sheets. I will give you only the gist of it. After recalling to Monsieur Février's memory the tragic story of the *Télémaque*, your brother urges him, in terms that are almost threatening, to leave town, in order to prevent a recurrence of scenes not only painful to himself but also prejudicial to Madame Canut's health. One such scene took place on the thirty-first of January, when you were at sea. Following her usual practice, your mother would not be shaken off, and Février had to take refuge in a shop."

"Your honor . . ." the lawyer began.

"No," Canut cut in almost angrily. "Let him say what he has to say."

"But . . ."

"This is my business, not yours." And, turning to the magistrate: "Go on, sir."

One of the queerest things in the whole queer affair was that, though so much was at stake in this interview, Canut caught himself listening to the whistles of the steamers moving in the river and even trying to calculate the state of the tide.

"On the evening following this painful scene at Fécamp, your brother wrote another letter, shorter than the first. This is what he says: 'I strongly advise you to leave Fécamp without more delay, and trust that this time my advice will have some effect.' In the light of the previous letter, I am forced to the conclusion that this note contains a threat, though, no doubt, a veiled one."

As if Charles were capable of using threats to anyone whatever!

"It was as a result of receiving this message, I presume, that Février sent that letter to you. He probably thought you would be more reasonable than your brother. The letter was handed to you at 8:00 P.M. on the second of February. At nine you were ringing the bell at the Villa des Mouettes, and we may assume that the interview began on a friendly tone, since your host offered you a drink. Nonetheless, you murdered him shortly afterward, and purloined the contents of a desk—valuable securities and cash to a total of about thirty thousand francs."

"Will your honor permit me to make an observation?" the lawyer began.

"Certainly, Maître Abeille. Certainly."

"I would be glad to learn what grounds you have for assuming that it was my client who . . ."

"That's enough!" growled Canut, scratching his head. It was clear to him that they'd gone about it the wrong way from the start, and might go on talking like this for hours without any good result. Yet, even if they'd started off on some different line, would it have been any better?

Everything seemed so unreal, like some absurd dream; this dreary office, the little lawyer, who now was smoking a cigarette, and the slight tingling of his wrists due to his moving his arms without remembering the handcuffs. Still, he'd better make an effort.

"Excuse me, sir. May I tell you exactly what happened?"

"Just a moment. I have some more questions to ask. After that you can have your say—though I doubt if, by then, it will serve any purpose. Do you admit that the jackknife used by the murderer to cut the victim's throat used to belong to your father and, indeed, has his initials on it?"

"Well, Février told me so."

"What did you say?"

"Février told me it had been my father's knife. He got it from a closet, and said I could keep it if I liked."

"Wait a minute! We'll come back to that later. . . . Take down that the prisoner admits the knife was . . ."

Abeille intervened. "May I point out, your honor, with all due deference, that my client has not admitted . . ."

Canut scowled at him. "He's right. I admitted it."

He had an instinctive dislike of the dapper little lawyer, and was quite capable of contradicting everything he said just to aggravate him.

"Two more questions, and that will be all for today. The police who searched your cabin found there a tobacco pouch of a rather unusual type. It's a pig's bladder with a string net around it, and the way the net is knotted shows that it was made by a sailor—so I am informed. Do you admit . . . ?"

"It was my father's tobacco pouch. At least, that's what Février told me."

"Has it always been in your possession?"

"No."

"When did it come into your hands?"

"Février gave it to me."

"On the night of his death? At the same time as he gave you the knife?"

To this Canut answered briefly, "Yes." The sooner it was over the better; his head was beginning to ache and he was longing to smoke.

"Now for my last question. Why, when the superintendent asked you if you'd been to see Monsieur Février, did you begin by saying you had not?"

Canut shrugged his shoulders wearily. "I had my reasons."

"What reasons?"

There was no reply. The examining magistrate turned to the lawyer. "You notice, Maître Abeille, that your client . . ."

Suddenly Canut seemed to wake out of a dream, and for the first time he raised his voice.

"Look! Can I have *my* say now, for a change?" He'd have liked to stand up, pace up and down the room and stretch his legs; and, most of all, get rid of the abominable handcuffs, whose presence he invariably forgot when he was making a gesture.

"It's quite short, what I have to say." His tone was surly. He had already guessed he was wasting his breath on these people; they wouldn't even try to follow. "When I came ashore that evening, Babette gave me a letter. The old fellow said he wanted me to come and see him, he had something important to tell me."

"Have you got the letter?"

"No."

"Will you tell us what you did with it?"

"How can I remember? What do you usually do with a letter after you've read it? Probably I tore it up and dropped it in the harbor."

"Go on with your story." For some reason the magistrate sounded pleased.

"I went to see him. I guessed that my mother had been making trouble again."

"Excuse me! Am I to infer that you did not share your mother's feelings toward the deceased?"

Canut stared at him, frowning.

"Do you refuse to answer my question?"

He all but retorted: Why should I answer a damn-fool question like that? In any case, his ideas on the subject

51

were vague, perhaps deliberately vague; what he and his brother had always wanted most of all was to keep their minds off the tragedy that had taken place before they were born and had clouded all their youth.

"Shall I go on?"

"Certainly, if you wish."

"Well, I went to the villa—without telling my brother."

"Why not?"

"Because he's not a seaman."

"I don't understand."

"I'm sorry. You would, if . . . No, it's no good explaining. But I thought that we'd better have things out, old Février and I, between ourselves—man to man, you know. Charles, my brother, has never been to sea; he wouldn't see things like we do. Well, he asked me in and we went into the living room. Then he offered me a drink."

"And you, the son of the man who died in the *Télémaque's* boat, consented to drink with . . . ?"

"That's my business. Don't talk about things you don't understand." He fell silent. It seemed so futile, trying to explain matters to these landsmen. Still, now that he'd started, there seemed no point in stopping halfway. "I repeat, we were talking man to man. Then, all of a sudden, Février told me he'd decided to move and was going to sell his house."

"To whom?"

"I didn't ask him. It was none of my business."

"If I asked you that, it was because, though we have looked through all his correspondence, we have found nothing to show that the house was going to be sold. . . . Very well. What else have you to tell me?"

Just then he heard again two short, shrill whistles from a boat that was going down the Seine and would be in the open sea by nightfall, and he fell to wondering if the tide would help her. . . .

The magistrate's voice broke through his musings. "Get on with your story."

"Do you think it's of the slightest use?"

"You heard what his honor said," the lawyer put in.

Canut gave him a long look, as if to say: "You, little man, are beginning to get on my nerves." Then he continued, with a sigh: "So Février told me all about it."

"About what?"

"About what happened when the *Télémaque* went down. And his experiences afterward. He told me that my father—he was quite young at the time—began to break down after . . . after what happened with the English sailor."

"'What happened with the English sailor'? Will you explain, please."

Canut shook his head. At the Villa des Mouettes, speaking "man to man," as he put it—as one seaman to another —he could talk about such things. But not here, not with that young ass Abeille staring at him, almost licking his lips at the prospect of a gruesome story, something he could retell dramatically, and now taking another cigarette from his case.

"Then he unlocked a drawer in his desk."

"The one, I presume, in which he kept his money and securities?"

"Maybe. I couldn't say. He took out a tobacco pouch, and then he got the knife and showed me the letters on it. These things were my father's, so he said. He swore that neither he nor any of the others had anything to do with my father's death. My father went crazy and cut a vein in his own wrist."

"And you believed him, I suppose?"

"Yes, I believed him."

"Then you went away, leaving the knife on the table?"

"That's right. I left in rather a hurry. What he'd been telling me had upset me, and, if you want to know, I threw up as soon as I was out of the house."

"Did Monsieur Février tell you he would be leaving Fécamp?"

"Yes. In two days' time, he said."

"Did he say where he meant to go?"

"No. But I gathered he thought of returning to South America, where he'd spent a good part of his life."

"And then you went straight home?"

"Yes."

"Did you pass anyone on the way?"

"I don't know. I didn't notice."

And then the examining magistrate bent forward, fixed his eyes sternly on Canut, and for the first time raised his voice. "Now then! Out with it! Where have you hidden the wallet containing Février's money?"

Canut stiffened, and remained motionless for a few moments. Then he slowly relaxed and stared gloomily at the floor.

"Answer me!"

Canut gave no sign of having heard.

"Ah? So you refuse to answer, do you?"

Canut had said it under his breath. But the others heard the word as distinctly as if he'd raised his voice, so complete was the silence except for a faint scratching from the clerk's pen.

Looking sideways at the wall, Canut had muttered: "Shit!"

# 4

WHEN ON Thursday, two days later, at eleven in the morning, Charles Canut got off the train at Fécamp, he felt like a changed man. The change came home to him most vividly at the moment when, on leaving the station, he had his first view of the harbor, veiled in rain and spray, the dingy cobblestone dock, the little houses straggling up narrow streets—in a word, Fécamp, his hometown, which until now he had taken so easily for granted.

But then he began to wonder: Had he really changed so much? Probably not. He couldn't have, if he'd tried. He was still a semi-invalid, overserious for his years, "a bit of a wet blanket," as he'd heard a friend describe him. No, what had changed was his surroundings, or, rather, his outlook on them.

Until now, these had been as obvious, as simple as the illustrations in a child's picture book. To begin with, there was the little house in which it seemed a certainty he would spend the rest of his days, along with Pierre and his mother, and, perhaps, later on, Babette as well. Equally permanent had seemed his Aunt Lou and those Sunday afternoons when they had sat in the back parlor, with jam tarts cooling on a long white sideboard, and exchanged commonplace, affectionate remarks. It was like a second home, and at each visit his aunt would kiss him on both cheeks, murmuring as a matter of course: "And how's your poor mother today?"

No one ever mentioned the young sailor whose photograph adorned the living room at Charles's home. By now he was forgotten, so many years had passed since his death. Still, they could never quite forget that they were an unlucky family, poor but respectable—for no one had a word to say against them; which was a consolation in a way.

Apart from Aunt Lou and their immediate neighbors, people one met daily at the same places, no one really counted in their lives except Monsieur Pessart, who couldn't deny that Pierre was far and away his best skipper, even if he did make schoolboyish spelling mistakes in his log. Then, of course, there was the railway company, a vaguely beneficent organization that hovered protectively around Charles—a comforting thought when, as so often happened, he was feeling low, uncertain of himself.

But now, it seemed, the bottom had dropped out of the world he knew, though how or why Charles had no clear idea. Even the houses seemed different; there was something almost hostile in their aspect, and he eyed them with mistrust. And when he entered the freight station, he felt like an outsider; the presence of Filloux at his desk, in the office where he worked, seemed to change the whole atmosphere of the little room.

"Well?" asked Filloux, in the tone one uses when addressing people who are in trouble.

"Yes?"

"What news of your brother?"

"He's still in jail." Charles announced it almost truculently, looking Filloux straight in the eyes. Then he continued, in a matter-of-fact voice: "Well, you can continue here for some time yet. I'm putting in for my yearly vacation immediately, and if they refuse, I shall take it just the same."

It was no vain boast. The meek and gentle Charles Canut of the past was gone; he now was capable of much more than this, if they drove him to it!

The events of the previous day were mainly responsible for the change that had come over him. In the morning, he had returned to the Law Courts, and instead of telling him that Pierre was in the examining magistrate's office, they had given evasive answers. Otherwise he'd have waited in the corridor until his brother came out.

However, to his surprise, when he was having his coffee after luncheon, a police inspector had come to see him at the hotel and told him he was wanted at the Law Courts immediately. Nevertheless, he was made to wait again—apparently they did it on principle—in the corridor, where the same doorkeepers (how he had come to loathe them) were chatting and smoking outside the various offices.

At last a voice called: "Canut, Charles!" He rose. A door opened. He found himself in an ordinary-looking office, rather like Monsieur Pessart's, and he saw his brother, still in oilskins, seated in a chair with his back to the window.

Neither of the brothers could have explained why he failed to show any emotion. Pierre looked up, and seemed to find it quite natural that his brother should be there.

Charles stopped in front of the desk, and as he turned toward the magistrate his eyes fell on Maître Abeille, who was smiling happily.

"Your name in full, please. Your occupation . . ."

It was at this stage that he began to question all his previous ideas about himself and the world at large. He realized that, for these people, he was just a vague, de-personalized nonentity, who happened to have the name Canut, and from whom they hoped to glean some information. He had ceased to be Charles Canut of Fécamp, who had studied so hard to acquire what knowledge lay within his grasp and devoted himself to building up his brother into the man he now was. And it was at this moment that the change set in. . . .

"My first question is: When did you see your brother last?"

"When the police arrested him."

"Yes. But before that?"

Charles realized that Monsieur Laroche was only doing his duty. He had a pleasant manner, and in private life was probably quite a likable man. And yet, sitting there with his well-kept hands flat on the documents in front of him, his head bent slightly forward, a look of calm interrogation in his eyes, he seemed to embody the utmost inhumanity of which civilized man is capable.

Charles didn't dare turn and throw a questioning glance at Pierre, and the silence lengthened until he felt he must break it at all costs.

"Well, I saw him the evening when the *Centaur* came in the time before."

"The second of February, you mean?"

"Perhaps. I don't remember exactly."

Strangely enough, Pierre didn't seem to be listening. And suddenly Charles caught sight of the handcuffs—and actually felt a twinge in his own wrists. He hastily averted his eyes.

"What time was it you saw him?"

What were they getting at? he wondered. Was there some trap in that question?

"I ask you," the magistrate repeated, "at what time you saw the prisoner on the night of the second of February."

"I've forgotten."

"About midnight, was it?"

It was on the tip of his tongue to answer "No." Then it struck him that Pierre might have said the contrary.

"I'm afraid I can't remember."

"Where did you see him?"

"Where? I've forgotten that, too."

"Did you know that he intended to visit Monsieur Février?"

What answer should he give? After a pause he shook his head. "No."

"And didn't he tell you about this visit next day?"

"No."

"May I take it that you saw him that morning, before he sailed?"

"No."

For the first time it dawned on him that all these trivial, everyday acts and events had been tremendously important, though at the time he'd had no inkling of it.

"Did you hear your brother come back that night?"

"No."

He'd been asleep, of course. How could he possibly have guessed that his being asleep that night was to have such weighty consequences?

"Did you tell your brother about the two letters you wrote to Monsieur Février?"

"No."

"Did you go to see Monsieur Février?"

"No."

He had reached the stage of being incapable of answering anything but "No," whatever they might ask him. Actually, he hardly knew what he was saying. It was like living in a nightmare, and the people in the room had the frowning immobility of the figures one sometimes sees in dreams.

Even Pierre in his oilskins, with his high, stubborn forehead, looked larger than life, a monstrous effigy hewn from somber granite. Abeille, the lawyer, still had his sickly smile, but it was the smile one sees on a waxwork figure, and his sleek hair might have been a wig. As for the magistrate, he was a mere wraith, sometimes vanishing completely behind the smoke of his cigarette.

"Do you admit that you and your brother were brought

up in—how shall I put it?—in a tradition of hatred of the late Février?"

He mumbled something and a moment later had forgotten what he'd said. Then he was made to sign a paper covered with writing. At the last moment he turned to look at Pierre, who was still seated with his hands on his knees. Pierre returned his gaze in silence.

That was the end. The doorkeeper was there. Charles went down flights of stairs strewn with cigarette butts.

Ever since then he had been brooding over that macabre experience, trying to dispel the odious impression it had left. Even Pierre had seemed different, and it was all he could do to picture him as he really was and recall the sound of his voice.

They hadn't used any threats, but there had been something insidious about those questions, almost more disquieting than threats. It had been like one of those sea fogs that come on very slowly but end up by blanketing the town, seeping into every cranny. The only positive impression he had gathered was that they'd trapped his brother and were out to trap him, too. Hadn't the magistrate hinted at this, and as good as warned him that he was under police surveillance until further notice?

So there was nothing for it but to face the facts, and recognize that the old way of life was gone. From now on he must stop being humble, self-effacing, eager to oblige; he must learn to be tough.

He was walking on the waterfront and already his expression had changed, grown harder. So intently was he gazing in front of him that he failed to notice a friend who passed quite close.

Fog or no fog, his job was clear; it was he who must rescue Pierre from the clutches of those people, and there was no one but himself to do it. Theoretically, no doubt, Abeille was on Pierre's side, but Charles had a feeling that in fact the lawyer was in the enemy's camp. Well, he'd see it through alone.

By now he was nearly home. He could already see the brightly polished door knocker, the curtains in the only window on the street. The door was green; he had painted it himself. And he, too, had installed running water, since he liked doing jobs around the house in his spare time. Only—the Charles now coming home was not the mild young man who had done those jobs; it was a different man altogether.

Three doors away was the Lachaume pastry shop, its window ranged with marble slabs on which only a few cakes were displayed; its door, when opened, set a bell tinkling that had a sound like no other shop bell in town.

When he entered, the shop was empty. As usual at this hour, his uncle was in the bakery, on the other side of the yard. After a moment his cousin came out of the back parlor; she was wearing a white apron.

"Oh, you're back, are you?" The vague question implied, he guessed, a host of others.

"How's Mother?"

"She caught a cold going out in the rain yesterday, and she's in bed. Mama's with her."

Just as well, perhaps, Charles thought; it might be better if his mother stayed in bed for a day or two.

"What are people here saying?" He gave Berthe a searching, almost suspicious, look.

"Oh, nothing much. Of course, nobody believes for a moment that Pierre could have done a thing like that. . . . Won't you have a snack, now you're here? . . . Excuse me, I must go to the kitchen; I have something on the fire."

She had looked at him in a new way, almost as if she was afraid of him, and this pleased Charles, because it showed that she had recognized the change in him. He left the shop, followed by another tinkle of the little bell, and went home. Letting himself in with his key, he went into the living room, a room that was seldom used and always smelled of linoleum.

Against one of the walls was a small piano, which

Charles had recently bought with his savings. He had always wanted to play the piano, not to impress others but because he genuinely liked music. But he had taken only six or seven lessons, and could play only the simplest pieces.

"Is that you, Berthe?" It was his aunt calling from the top of the stairs.

"No. It's me. I'm coming up."

But he lingered a moment to take a general look around, like someone visiting a house for the first time. It was as if he wanted to readjust his scale of values.

The hall had a tiled floor, and the walls were papered to imitate marble. At the end was a glass door leading to the kitchen, which, like the living room, was rarely used, because the floor above was so much warmer.

The steps creaked. There was a special, rather musty smell; Charles couldn't have described it, since his home had always had that smell. And the aunt who stood waiting for him on the landing also had a special smell, a rather nasty one—so much so, indeed, that as a small boy he had always avoided kissing her.

"Pierre?" she whispered.

He shook his head; then asked: "Does Mother know?"

She nodded.

"Who told her?"

"Nobody. She seemed to have guessed. . . ."

A voice came from a bedroom: "Is that you, Charles?"

His heart sank as he entered; it was as if he realized the family disaster in its entirety for the first time, now that he had to face his mother.

"Good morning, Mother."

As he bent to kiss her forehead, he noticed that her eyes were dry and calm; evidently she was in a lucid phase. Then a new, surprising, thought stopped him. "How young she is!" For today he was looking at people and things as if he had just returned from a long journey—though actually he had been absent only two days.

"Have you seen him?" He was struck by the childishness of her voice. It was like that of a little girl who is afraid of being scolded.

Still, that was no great change really; she was always like this between her "attacks." She effaced herself as much as possible, and seemed to be begging forgiveness of those around her for all the trouble she caused them.

"Yes, I've seen him."

"Are they going to keep him there?"

"They won't keep him long," he said firmly. "I'll see to that."

She began to whimper, and her eyes grew teary.

"It's all my fault. But I know, I *know* Pierre didn't kill that man. Charles! . . . Pierre! . . . My darlings!"

She often called her sons to her when she felt an attack coming on, and seemed to find some consolation in their nearness.

"Pierre! I swear I never meant . . ."

"If you don't mind," Aunt Lou put in, "I'll run around to my place for a moment."

"Certainly," Charles said.

"Pierre! No, it's Charles. . . . I must go and see that magistrate. He'll believe me; I know he will."

The bed was the one bought when she set up house with her husband; the crocheted bedspread was one she had made during her brief married life. To the right of the bed was a big wardrobe with a mirror; the wallpaper had a cheerful pattern of red and yellow flowers, among which Charles, when he was a small boy, used to imagine he saw his father's face, if he half closed his eyes.

"Try to sleep, Mother. Pierre won't be in jail long, I promise you. By the way, I must send him some clothes this afternoon."

He would have to ask Aunt Lou to continue looking after his mother. He wouldn't have time for it; also, it would get on his nerves—and he urgently needed to keep a clear head today. Anyhow, there was no need to take the situation, as far as his mother was concerned, overtragically; she had been having these attacks ever since he could remember. The important thing was that somebody be with her to prevent her getting up, because she might want to at any moment.

"Now, Mother, you mustn't fret. Everything will be quite all right in a day or two. I'll get you something to eat now."

"You'll find some ham. And Aunt Lou brought a tart."

It wasn't only mentally that she had remained a young girl; physically, too, she had never grown up. Her development seemed to have been arrested when she was twenty and the news came to her of her husband's death. It struck Charles now that, in a sense, his mother was little older than Babette! And his father, too, was much younger, almost a boy in fact, when he, Charles, was born.

Yet his mother had had two children and, almost single-handed, kept the home together. She was slim, pale-cheeked, always dressed in black. On the rare occasions when she smiled, her mouth had a curious twist. . . .

"Charles!"

"Yes, Mother?" he called from the room that served as a kitchen.

"Eat all the ham. You need to keep up your strength." She emphasized the "you."

She was always telling them to keep up their strength and never thought about her own, though she had next to none. And yet somehow she was seldom ill in the ordinary sense.

"Don't forget to pack your brother's flannel shirts," she reminded him.

In each of the other houses in the little town people were gathering around a table for their meal. At the Canuts' house they ate standing or seated, sometimes one after the other, and ate cold dishes for the most part.

There were footsteps on the stairs. It was Aunt Lou coming back, sooner than Charles had expected.

64

"Has she had anything to eat?"

"Not yet . . . I must go to the station now with Pierre's things."

He had resolved to concentrate his thoughts and energies entirely on the task at hand, and to go about it steadily, methodically. He dispatched the suitcase himself, and his fellow employees at the office were struck by his calmness—as he'd intended them to be.

Then, still following his program, he walked quickly to the Café de l'Amiral.

"Where's Babette?" Despite his efforts there was a shade of anxiety in his voice.

Jules looked him up and down.

"She's here. . . . Babette!"

"Coming," her voice called from a room at the back.

For a moment he felt uneasy; then he told himself she might quite well have jobs to do in the back room as well as in the café proper. A door opened. She took some steps forward, wiping her face with her sleeve, a duster in her hand.

"Oh, it's you. What news?"

"None. I've come back because . . ."

"What are they going to do with Pierre?"

"I don't know. . . . I've come here to find out the truth about Février's death. Bring me coffee, please."

When she brought it, he couldn't refrain from asking rather nervously: "Has Paumelle been in while I was away?"

"Paumelle? Wait a minute! Yes, I think he came last evening."

"Did he talk to you?"

"No. Well, just a word or two. Only to pass the time of day."

Convinced though he was that, to get any good results, he must clear his mind of these preoccupations, he somehow couldn't manage it all at once. He would have to break gradually with the old life.

"I've put in for a week's vacation," he told her.

"Oh, have you?"

Why at this moment did a picture rise before him of Babette living with them in the little house—with his mother, Pierre, and sometimes Aunt Lou? For some moments he was silent.

"What are you thinking about?" she asked.

"Nothing."

Nothing and everything! He was thinking of the queer way life turned out; of his mother, who had had two children when she was little older than Babette. He even found himself picturing Babette as a mother. Impatiently, he forced his thoughts back to the present.

"I'm going to draw my money out of the savings bank. And I will stick to it until I discover what really happened."

"Mightn't he have committed suicide?"

For a moment he toyed with this theory, then rejected it. Does a sane man kill himself by slitting his throat with a knife?

As if she'd read his thoughts, Babette added: "You remember that Algerian who killed himself last year? He cut his throat with a razor."

No. Any theory of suicide was ruled out in Février's case. Money and valuables had been stolen. He shook his head.

"Février didn't kill himself," he said decisively.

Now what was that odd question the magistrate had asked him? Yes, now he remembered, though at the time it hadn't made much impression, unexpected though it was. "Did your brother own a jackknife engraved with his initials?" He certainly had answered "No." Pierre owned no such knife. Then came the other question: "Have you ever seen him using a tobacco pouch made of a pig's bladder encased in netting?"

He'd scratched his head. He'd had a vague memory of such a pouch, but couldn't place it. Now it came back to him. Besides the enlarged photograph hanging in the living room, they had three small snapshots of his father, and he and his brother had several times examined them with a magnifying glass. In one of these his father was in the act of filling his pipe, and he was using a pouch of a peculiar kind, corresponding to the one described by the magistrate.

He couldn't remember what answer he had given. Anyhow, it was a mean trick to spring such questions on a person without a word of explanation; and it didn't matter how he'd answered.

Another thing he'd been asked was: "Do you know if the deceased had any enemies, apart from members of your family?"

Just then Jules called Babette, who promptly got up. It was always like that. They never could have ten minutes' chat in peace. And now Jules took Babette's place, sitting astride the chair with his elbows on the back—his favorite posture—and sucking at an old meerschaum pipe.

"Well, young fellow?"

Charles resented being thus addressed, but took care not to betray his feelings.

"I don't suppose you know," Jules continued, "but the cops are still coming here off and on. Looks like they don't feel too sure about the case, don't it? Only last evening the super was here again, and he stayed in that chair you're sitting in till close to midnight."

"Did he ask you anything?"

"We had a little talk, him and me, earlier in the day."

"What did you tell him?"

Charles rather disliked Jules, though he really had nothing against him except that he was Babette's employer and, as such, might feel free to take liberties with her.

"I told him that your brother hadn't the stuff to do a thing like that. It wouldn't be like him; he's too soft. Know what I mean?"

Charles knew very well, and he knew that Jules was right. With all his bulk and tough appearance, Pierre was the most tender-hearted of men; he couldn't even bring himself to kill a rabbit for dinner.

"And I told him that if any member of your family did for the old boy, it was more likely to have been you." Jules's eyes settled on Charles, and the look was that of someone who has seen life in many aspects and learned to size men up. "That's so, ain't it?"

"Neither of us did it."

"You're bound to say that, of course—but I assume it's the truth. . . . Some people here say they won't stand for it if Pierre ain't let out in a day or two. And I wouldn't be surprised if there's trouble when the *Centaur* comes in again."

A short silence followed. Jules pushed his chair back a few inches and gave a heave to his trousers, which kept slipping down his paunch.

"Well, what's your idea about it?"

"My idea?" Charles repeated. He wasn't really sure if he trusted the café proprietor.

"I'll bet there's someone you suspect."

And promptly Charles's eyes shifted toward the table at which Paumelle usually sat. Jules chuckled.

"Aye; you see, I was right. But let me tell you, that boy's no fool, and you'll have to go about it carefully."

It was the slack hour. No one was in the taproom, and Babette was doing the washing up; he had glimpses of her through the kitchen doorway, with a plate or a glass in her hand.

"Suppose," Jules continued, "you start by finding out where he's been living since his father died. As a matter of fact, I had a word with the Twister about it. You know who I mean? That fellow who was the old one's deck hand; he sometimes comes here for a pint. Mind you, I'm not hinting at anything. All I'm concerned with is to see that people spend their money here. If all my customers were like you, young man, who stay a whole night over a cup of coffee, I'd do better to shut up shop. Paumelle at least stands a round of drinks now and then—when he's flush."

"Did you tell that to the superintendent?"

"No. He didn't ask me. Anyhow, it's none of my business; it's yours. . . ."

"Look! Do you know something?"

"No, I don't. And, mind you, don't go telling people that I've put you on to anything. I'd swear I hadn't, if you did. We just had a little talk—that's all. Février's been back in Fécamp for some time, and Paumelle may have got to know him."

There was an interruption. The coastguardsman and a shipbuilder who had a yard nearby had dropped in for a game of cards. The lock keeper was sent for to make a fourth, and, after laying a cloth on a table, Jules began to shuffle the pack. Charles remained in his corner, staring at the floor.

He could hear the cardplayers talking about his brother and himself in undertones between hands, but he preferred to fix his mind on what he'd just been told.

How could he hope to discover anything by himself? Yet it seemed equally hopeless to do what to his mind was the obvious thing: go to the superintendent and advise him to keep an eye on young Paumelle.

"My brother," he could have added, "is a perfectly honorable man; you have only to ask people here what they think of him. He would never dream of doing harm to anyone. But Paumelle's a ne'er-do-well, a fellow who spends three nights a week in the brothels. And that costs money, which he certainly doesn't earn by the odd jobs one sees him doing now and then." Jules, who's a shrewd fellow, is quite right, he thought. It would be worth finding out how he gets that money.

He beckoned to Babette, paid, and left the café reluctantly; once outside, he lingered for a while, gazing gloomily at the harbor.

How could he find out if Paumelle and Février were acquainted? One thing seemed certain: they couldn't have met in any tavern, because Février never set foot in such places. Nor did he often venture into town, where there was always the risk of encountering Madame Canut.

It might be a good thing to look up Tatine, who had been Février's cleaning woman since he came to Fécamp. She lived near the Old Harbor with her sister, a dressmaker who sometimes worked for the Lachaumes.

Charles started off at a brisk pace, but as he approached the Old Harbor his self-confidence began to falter. How should he go about it? What could he say to the old woman? People who passed him turned to stare curiously; others greeted him with a "Good day." The clouds hung low, their grayness faintly yellowed by a hidden sun.

He had to go all the way along the waterfront; then cross some empty lots. After them came a row of tumbledown cottages, flanked by garbage dumps and patches of nettles. In the first of these cottages lived the organist who had given him piano lessons.

In the cottage two doors farther on a sewing machine was purring. Evidently it was here that Tatine's sister lived. Charles knocked boldly on the door, but when he heard slippered feet shuffling up the hall, his nervousness increased.

An old woman in a blue-and-white-checked apron, with white hair and sallow cheeks, opened the door. It was Tatine. The moment she saw Charles, she quickly pushed the door to, except for a gap of a few inches.

"What do you want?" she asked in a quavering voice.

"I'd like to have a word with you. It's most important. Please let me in."

She turned and shouted down the hall: "Jeanne! Come here a moment."

The sewing machine stopped. Another old woman came into the hall, and asked mistrustfully: "Who is it?"

"It's his brother. What shall I do?"

The two old women talked in whispers behind the door, which they seemed to regard as a defense, though Charles could easily have pushed it wide open and walked in.

"I won't keep you long," Charles said. "Do please listen to what I have to say."

"You can let him in, dear. It'll be all right, I think. I work at his aunt's. . . ."

They shepherded him into a small room on the right. The table was strewn with squares of cloth and canvas on which were pinned old colored patterns.

"Well, Monsieur Canut, what do you want?" Tatine asked nervously.

The two women kept very close together, gazing at him apprehensively, as if they expected him to attack them at any moment. Through the curtains the Old Harbor could be seen, with derelict boats moldering on the foreshore.

"My brother is innocent. Everyone knows that." His voice was firm, decided. "And I will prove it to the police. But first I must find out who the murderer was."

The sisters exchanged glances, as if asking each other: Did you ever hear anything like that?

Lowering his eyes, Charles went on speaking, but in a less assured tone, for their attitude disconcerted him.

"If Monsieur Février was murdered, it was by somebody else, not by my brother. And it must have been somebody who knew him."

Tatine folded her hands on her stomach, like a bishop in a stained-glass window, and her expression conveyed her feelings all too clearly. It was as if she were saying in so many words: Talk away, young man, but you'll get nothing out of me!

"What I'd really like to know," Charles continued, "is who visited Monsieur Février in the last few weeks before his death. For instance, was there anyone in particular who knew his way around the house and . . ."

"You should ask the police those questions, young man."

"But . . ."

"When that policeman questioned me, I didn't keep a thing back. The law's the law, and he was in his rights. But as for you . . . well, I must say you have some nerve coming and badgering decent folks like this, folks that ain't done nothing to you." She glanced at her sister, who nodded approval. "And if it wasn't that your auntie's a real nice woman, I wouldn't have opened the door to you."

"Anyhow, you might tell me just one thing. Does Gaston Paumelle . . . ?"

"Not another word, young man. We've no reason to tell you nothing, and you won't get nothing out of us, and that's straight. Not to mention that likely as not you'll be in jail tomorrow or the next day."

Inwardly quaking at their temerity, the two old crones shuffled forward a few steps, hustling Charles back toward the doorway. He made a last attempt.

"I hate to bother you, but can't you realize that . . . ?"

"Marthe, step outside, will you? If he refuses to go away, call for help."

Unthinkingly he murmured, "Sorry," put on his cap, and started walking straight ahead, in the rain.

# 5

EVERYONE CONCERNED was acting according to his lights, so to speak, and viewing the case from his own angle. Thus Monsieur Laroche, who was entertaining friends that evening, was airing his views to his guests at the dinner table. Cheese had just been served, and he was sniffing his glass of Chambertin with the gusto of a connoisseur. An Appeals judge and his wife were dining with him; also an old friend from Tahiti, where he was chief prosecutor.

"He's a rather puzzling type of man. Sometimes I see him as a hulking, callous brute, without any feelings at all. But there are moments when I wonder if he isn't really a simple sort of fellow, with an undeveloped mind, who suffers from our old friend the 'inferiority complex.' I've tried several methods of approach."

Monsieur Laroche came from Chalon-sur-Saône and his wife from Mâcon, and they were reputed to have one of the best cellars in Rouen.

"I'm rather reluctant to have his mother brought here; she's an invalid, it seems, and has to stay in bed. So I suppose I will have to go to Fécamp tomorrow to examine her."

He was wrong. At the time he was speaking, Madame Canut was up and about; she had sent her sister home and, with a poultice around her neck, was busy tidying up the house despite the lateness of the hour. It may be that she expected Pierre's return at any moment. Or could she have had an intuition that the magistrate intended to call on her?

Meanwhile, Maître Abeille was at the theater, where a gala night was in progress, with a company from Paris. He was practically the only man in full evening dress, but this didn't embarrass him in the least. On the contrary, he was very much in evidence in the corridors during the intermissions, buttonholing acquaintances and imparting the latest news of the Fécamp murder case.

"No, you're wrong there. It's quite in the cards that the trial will be held at the present Assizes. The preliminary inquiry will be over in a day or two. It's a queer case, quite the most dramatic one we've had for years. Not the murder itself, but what lies behind it. Just picture to yourself those men adrift in an open boat for weeks and weeks . . ."

Superintendent Gentil was rolling a cigarette every five or ten minutes, lighting it, taking a sip of beer, and trying to overhear the conversations going on around him. He came from Raincy, where he had lived for forty years; then for fifteen years he had been in Paris, in the special brigade attached to the Presidency.

Here at Fécamp he was out of his depth. Everything conspired to baffle him: the local accent, to his ears unintelligible; the lack of curiosity these people showed about him; and even the queer smell pervading the café, in which raw gin predominated.

He had settled down for the evening in the Amiral, and everyone knew who he was. Nevertheless, no one looked his way; indeed, his presence was ignored. He had come here out of a sense of duty. Because, though convinced of Pierre Canut's guilt, he was conscious that several points in the case needed clearing up, and it was only here that he had any chance of doing this.

Of all the people involved, the one who felt least sure of himself was Charles. Yet, while his thoughts kept turning in a seemingly hopeless circle, an idea was developing beneath the surface, an idea that almost had a touch of genius in it.

It had begun to germinate after his visit to the two old women. He had started by walking more or less blindly ahead, and when, after some minutes, he paused to take his bearings, he found he was quite near Février's house.

It struck Charles as odd that people had built their houses in such a remote, inconvenient place, on the far side of the harbor, instead of in the town. To get here they had to cross patches of muddy wasteland, and edge their way along a narrow, dimly lit path flanked by a high fence. Yet here, at the foot of the cliff, quite a number of small houses of the seaside-cottage type had been built. Pretty enough in an unpretentious way, and surrounded by small fenced-in gardens, they looked like the houses across the Channel on the English coast.

The road was only partly finished. There were not enough houses to form a continuous line, and those that were there had been placed, seemingly at random, at irregular intervals. Between them the road petered out into a mere track.

After a while Charles stopped. It had struck him that this was the place and the moment to reconstruct the scene on the night of Février's death. "Let's see now. It was close to midnight when Pierre came. There must have been a light on in the old man's house. Probably the cottages were dark."

Their occupants were, like Tatine, poor people who put up with the remoteness and inconvenience of the spot for the sake of the low rent.

Charles was not looking for anything in particular as he

ran his eyes carelessly over the little houses. But his attention was caught by one of them: it was different from the others. True, he knew of its existence, but he hadn't given it a thought until now. It was odd enough that a road should have been made to serve a few scattered cottages, grouped at some distance from the line of houses; and perhaps odder still that anyone should have thought of opening a café—or an *estaminet*, as the lettering across its solitary window described it—in a place like this.

Anyhow, there it was; as small and cramped as the little dwellings near it, but blatantly new, flaunting embroidered curtains, a makeshift bar, and two small tables, surrounded not by ordinary café chairs but by deal stools, plain but very highly polished.

Charles had never set foot in the *estaminet*. But he knew that it was owned by a Flemish woman whom everyone called Emma. She had come here as a war refugee and stayed on.

She must be almost fifty now, Charles supposed. Though her establishment was not actually a place of ill repute, it had none too savory a reputation. The men who visited it rarely came in groups, and there were never any games of cards or dominoes, as in other cafés. Nor did Emma's customers go there to drink. Behind the counter there were never more than a few bottles of a cheap brand of beer, one of brandy, and another containing chocolate liqueur—the only drink that Emma personally fancied.

The place was patronized chiefly by elderly men, widowers or bachelors who found time hanging heavy on their hands. After strolling along the waterfront, watching boys fishing and boats coming in or going out, they would stop in at the little café, whose homely air appealed to them.

"How are you today, Emma?"

"I'm fine. How about you? Any news of your daughter?"

Emma knew all about her customers' private lives, and

often gave them sound advice when they told their troubles to her. She was a restful person. At whatever time of day one came, she could always be found crocheting, in thick wool of the gaudiest colors.

"Help yourself, dear. And while you're up, you might fetch me a glass of the usual"—meaning the chocolate liqueur.

They would stay for hours chatting beside the stove, on which a kettle simmered, while the clock on the mantelpiece chimed the quarter-hours. There were some visitors who wanted more than these mild conversations—two or three at least, so the story went. When one of them came, Emma would bolt the door and, some minutes later, let down the blind of her bedroom window.

Charles realized that if any of his friends saw him right now, he would be hard put to it to account for his lingering here, gazing vaguely at the *estaminet*. Actually, a definite idea, which might well lead to something, had entered his mind. Suppose that Emma had kept her place open, as she might well have, until midnight on that eventful night of February second. In that case, Pierre might have been seen by someone there when he was walking past, on his way to Février's house. Also, that person, whoever he was, might have had his curiosity aroused and waited until he saw Pierre leaving.

True, he had no clear notion what discoveries this might lead to, but at least it provided him with a start, a working hypothesis that he might well put to the test. His gaze roved to the house eighty yards away, then back to the little café. One thing was certain: whenever Février took a stroll he was bound to pass Emma's door. Though over sixty, he carried his years well. Wasn't he, in fact, just the sort of elderly man who enjoys having a chat, and perhaps something more, with a woman like Emma?

What made this all the likelier was Février's past; he had "seen trouble," as they say. And he certainly wouldn't feel inclined to unburden himself to that hag of a cleaning woman, Tatine. The Flemish refugee, on the other hand, was just the sort of confidante he would appreciate.

Obviously Charles's first task was to find out if Février was in the habit of visiting the café. Without stopping to think out a method of approach, Charles crossed the road. A small bell tinkled as he opened the door. Emma was at her usual place beside the window, with the curtain drawn some inches to one side so she had only to raise her eyes to see who came along the road.

"Good day." She rose from her chair reluctantly. "What'll you have to drink?"

"I don't know . . . yes, a glass of beer, please."

He was conscious of being clumsy. He wasn't used to handling such situations. The table at which he was seated was up against a wall, and above it hung a garish color print of one of the French kings quaffing beer from a tankard rimmed with lightning.

"Here you are." After giving him his drink, she returned to her chair and paid no more attention to Charles. Some instinct told him he had come on a fool's errand.

In spite of her age and bulk, Emma still had a certain attractiveness, and there was something statuesque about her—one felt she was capable of remaining seated, as she now was, for the whole day, counting the chain aloud as she plied her crochet hook.

"Do many people come here?" Charles blushed as he spoke; his voice sounded so strained and unnatural.

She replied without looking up from her work: "Now and then. It depends."

He was aware that a certain subtlety was called for; a well-phrased question might elicit some really useful information. Only too well he knew his awkwardness, but he was determined to see it through, even at the cost of making himself ridiculous.

"I suppose the people who live around here drop in pretty often?"

"Some of 'em."

"Of course, it's much handier for them to come here than go all the way down to town when they want a drink."

"That's so."

Did she know who he was? Charles couldn't be sure. He was much less well known than his brother. On the other hand, he resembled Pierre, and there had been pictures of Pierre in the newspapers.

"Do they play games here in the evenings?"

"Games? What sort of games?"

"Oh, you know what I mean. Dominoes, cards, and so on."

"Sometimes."

Her taciturnity was wearing him down, but he forced himself to go on talking.

"It's the best way of spending an evening for people who can't get to sleep early. I'm like that; I never can get a wink of sleep till midnight at the earliest."

At last she raised her eyes and looked at him, but it was impossible to guess what, if anything, was in her mind.

"Now that I come to think of it," Charles continued doggedly, "I believe I've seen your lights on here quite late at night."

"Yes?" she murmured vaguely; then resumed her crocheting.

There was a longish silence, broken only by a ripple of chimes from the clock. During the next quarter of an hour Charles was so much absorbed in his thoughts that when the clock chimed again, he was almost startled to see where he was.

"How much do I owe you?"

"Ninety centimes."

On the point of leaving, he changed his mind. There was no precise reason; he acted on intuition.

"After all, I think I'll have another glass."

With a sigh she rose and served him. Then she put a shovelful of coal in the stove, adjusted the flue, and, seeing that her customer showed no sign of making a move, retired to a room at the back, where she could be heard grinding coffee.

Thus Charles was by himself when the door opened abruptly. The man who entered was none other than Paumelle, who stopped short and looked at Charles with undisguised astonishment.

"Well, I'm damned!" he muttered.

Charles, who was equally surprised, did his best to keep an impassive face.

Paumelle was in his usual attire: blue work pants, a sweater, clogs. Long strands of brownish hair straggled out from beneath his checked cap, and he deliberately exaggerated his tough-guy manner, thrusting his hands deep in his pockets, letting his cigarette dangle from his lower lip, and squaring his shoulders as he strutted across the room.

"Are you there, Emma?" he called, and without waiting for an answer entered the back room, slamming the door behind him. The sound of the coffee mill stopped, but, though Charles heard their voices, he couldn't make out what was being said.

He had half a mind to leave. For one thing, he knew he was no use if it came to a fight, and Paumelle had a notorious penchant for roughhousing.

Nevertheless, he stayed—though he could feel cold sweat on his arms and chest—if only to convince himself that, when necessary, he could play the hero. Meanwhile, he planned his tactics; if Paumelle went for him, the best thing would be to fend him off with the legs of a chair, and he made sure there was a chair within easy reach.

They were still talking in the other room, in what seemed ordinary tones. The door opened. Emma had come to fetch the coffeepot, and she gave Charles no more than a casual glance. But this time the door was left ajar.

Charles heard boiling water being poured on the coffee, then Paumelle's voice.

"Anything to eat?"

"Yes. Look on the sideboard. There's a bun left from this morning."

Emma appeared again and placed two yellow earthenware mugs on the table at which she had been working; then she went back to the kitchen and returned with a coffeepot and a sugar bowl. Munching his bun, Paumelle slouched in, and stopped for a moment in front of Charles, eying him truculently. Then he sat down beside the Flemish woman and swung his feet up on a chair.

"What're you doing here?" he asked Charles. "I've heard there's a cell empty in the Rouen jail and they're keeping it nice and warm for you."

Evidently Emma understood this, because she bestowed on Charles a broad smile, the smile of a fat, rather stupid woman who relishes a joke, however feeble, at someone else's expense.

Paumelle turned to her. "You ain't put chicory in the coffee, I hope."

"You know quite well I never use chicory in the afternoon."

"So you say. Here! Put some sugar in for me. Show us today's paper—there's something I want to see."

Docilely she rose, brought a newspaper from behind the counter, and handed it to him. Thrusting the last piece of bun into his mouth, he lit a cigarette and opened the paper. He read while stirring his coffee with his left hand.

Some minutes passed, each seeming twice its normal length. The clock ticked vigorously, but the hands moved so sluggishly that one could have fancied them half stuck to the dial. A crane was at work on the far side of the harbor, and the rattle of its chains made a background of intermittent sound, and now and again a steamer tooted, or a door slammed in a neighboring cottage.

"Get me more coffee!"

Charles had never been so ill at ease; he had been staring at the beer-quaffing monarch on the wall so long that it made him feel quite squeamish. Still, he'd made a discovery of sorts, which might lead to something: that Paumelle was a frequent visitor to Emma's, perhaps her lover. Certainly the way he was behaving implied this. And his attitude toward Charles implied: You've seen what you wanted to! Does it help any? Well, now that you've done your stuff, the best thing you can do is to clear out and leave us in peace.

Nevertheless, Charles did not clear out. He was resolved to see it through—though of what he meant by "it" he had no very clear idea—even if it meant a fight with Paumelle.

"By the way, Emma, did you do what I told you? About putting flypaper on the chairs?"

For a moment she looked puzzled; then she glanced at Charles and burst out laughing, so heartily that she nearly brought her coffee up.

"Oh, stop it!" she gurgled. "Don't make us laugh like that. I feel wet all over!" Her cheeks were deeply flushed, and her blue eyes streaming. Her voice, too, had changed, and Charles was struck by the thick Flemish accent.

Pleased with his success, Paumelle was chuckling, doubtless thinking up some other joke.

Paumelle was a love child, the son of a girl who had left Fécamp soon after his birth and was said to be now in a brothel somewhere in the South of France. She must have been a pretty girl, for Paumelle certainly did not get his looks from his father. He had well-molded features and, despite the loutish manner he affected, there was something in his carriage that suggested breeding.

"I have an idea, Emma. Run around to the photographer's and ask him to come along with his camera. We ought to have his photo on the wall to commemorate his visit. Perhaps he'd sign it if you asked him nicely."

Was Charles mistaken, or was there a note of apprehension in the young man's bluster, and even, perhaps, a hint of anger? Anyhow, he noticed, Paumelle wasn't reading his paper. He merely used it as a pretext for striking effective poses and indulging in long silences.

"Give us a spot of brandy, old thing. From *my* bottle, mind!"

It struck Charles that at this very moment at the Café de l'Amiral, Babette was serving drinks and enduring men's familiarities, and the thought had its usual depressing effect. . . .

At last Paumelle changed his position, and turning his back on Charles, began speaking in a low voice, almost a whisper, to Emma. He talked on and on, like someone with a lot of things to tell an old friend.

It upset Charles still more, having to listen to this faint murmur of conversation without being able to know what it was about. Probably Paumelle was talking on any subject that came into his head. But perhaps also of the one, the only one, that was of interest to Charles.

"Well, Emma, I'll be off. I would think he'll be here any time now."

It was six o'clock. Presumably Paumelle was referring to one of Emma's regular customers. As soon as the door closed behind Paumelle, Charles rose from his chair.

"Good night," he said, and got no answer.

Brief panic came over him when he saw Paumelle in the shadows just ahead, walking along the edge of the sea wall, slowing down now and then to step over the hawsers of the boats alongside. It was a lonely spot, and there were only two street lamps on the whole road, both on the other side. Charles had a sense of imminent danger. It would be the easiest thing for Paumelle to lie in wait, let Charles come along, and, with a quick lunge, send him spinning into the dark waters of the harbor. But he decided to take his chance; he wasn't going to beat a cowardly retreat. Still, as he walked ahead, he kept a wary eye on Paumelle, who, instead of continuing along the sea wall, turned off at the swing bridge and stopped for a moment halfway across to gaze down at the water.

Yes, Paumelle might well be Février's murderer. If so, he must be gloating over the turn events had taken. Because he hated Pierre with the special kind of hatred that sometimes exists within a family circle. There was the link between them that the fathers of both had belonged to the crew of the *Télémaque* on her last, ill-fated voyage, and even Charles had an absurd sense of kinship with Paumelle—almost as if he were a cousin who had gone bad.

When all was said and done, was young Paumelle wholly to blame? Perhaps not. His father had been a drunkard who let him roam the streets in rags and tatters. The only person to show any interest in the child was his father's deck hand, the Twister, a rather sinister personage, who indulged in such illegal practices as fishing with dynamite and stealing cod from railway cars. Everyone had as little truck with him as possible. And when his father died, Paumelle hadn't attended the funeral, but spent the day in a bar.

Probably he was jealous of the two other young men, of Pierre especially, who was captain of a ship and highly esteemed in the town; indeed, one got tired of hearing people singing his praises. If a stranger to the place inquired, "Who's that fellow, Pierre Canut?" the answer was sure to be: "Canut? He's the best skipper on the coast. And as straight as a die. He'll always give you a square deal; he'd rather be out of pocket than let a fellow down." When any dispute arose among the fishermen, someone was sure to suggest: "Why not call in Canut to settle it?" And, if some important decision had to be taken as regards the fishing fleet: "Let's wait and see what Canut has to suggest."

When they were little, he and Pierre, they were always

being given candy in the shops, and sometimes a worthy matron would sigh compassionately: "Poor little ones! They have an unhappy home."

Whereas everyone regarded Paumelle as a young hooligan and treated him accordingly.

Why, now, was he entering the Amiral? Just to irritate Charles, as likely as not. Going straight to the counter, he patted Babette playfully on the cheek.

"Hello, baby! By the way, my dog has followed me in—such a faithful creature, isn't he? What about giving him a drink?"

Paumelle slouched off to his usual seat, and Charles, who had heard every word, frowned, wondering how to act. Finally he sat down with his back to the wall, facing his enemy.

Babette didn't appear to have understood. She gave Charles a glance that seemed to ask him what it meant; then took the two young men's orders. As he was waiting for his drink, Charles noticed that Superintendent Gentil was sitting at the next table, only a yard or so away.

It struck him that for some perverse reason things never turned out as they should where he was concerned. Now, for instance, nothing could be simpler than for him to tell the superintendent about his suspicions and discoveries. And then the police officer could have got busy questioning people and eliciting the facts.

But no! He, Charles, had learned his lesson. Nothing would be gained by tackling the superintendent, who belonged to the same clan as the examining magistrate and Maître Abeille. . . . Meanwhile, Paumelle was showing off, throwing his weight around as usual. Just now he was giving unsolicited advice to some men playing cards at the table next to his.

"Have you sent your brother his clothes?"

Charles jumped, and turned toward the superintendent, who had addressed him in a quite amiable tone.

"Yes."

"It's all been rather hurried, of course. Did the magistrate let you see him?"

"Yes, but only for a moment."

The police officer gazed at him, crossed and uncrossed his legs, at a loss for anything more to say. After a while he sighed and murmured: "It must be terrible for your mother, I'm afraid. Does she realize what's happened?"

"Yes, she knows."

"Still, of course, we couldn't have acted otherwise."

He, too, didn't look particularly cheerful. He was no longer young, Charles noticed, and once, after making a wry face, he took a pillbox from his vest pocket and swallowed a couple of pills. Charles vaguely wondered what was wrong with him.

Jules, too, the owner of the Amiral, was a sick man; indeed, the doctor had warned him that unless he kept to a strict diet he wouldn't last out the year. Nonetheless, he had drinks with his customers off and on all day. In the mornings there were dark pouches under his eyes, his cheeks were gray and drawn, and he declared to anyone who happened to be around that he needed a big glass of gin to restore himself. After drinking it, he revived a little and some color came to his face.

"Have you gone back to work?" the superintendent asked.

"No."

This reminded Charles that he'd have to return to the station to find out whether they had granted him vacation leave or not. Not that it would make any change in his plans, one way or other.

Seeking him talking to the superintendent, Babette stayed in the background, and Charles had to call to her across the room.

"Give me something to eat, please. Bread and cold sausage will do, if there's nothing else."

"We have grilled herrings tonight."

"Good. Bring me a couple."

In the daytime, what with the boats coming in and putting out, the Café de l'Amiral was usually fairly full; at night, it was little more cheerful than Emma's. For one thing, like all the houses in town, even Monsieur Pessart's, it was dimly lighted. A grayish mist hovered around the filaments of the light bulbs: the air was full of tobacco smoke.

Two games of cards were in progress at tables spread with dingy red cloths blazoned with the trademark of the brewery that supplied them. Not far from Charles, two elderly dominoes enthusiasts were making an irritating intermittent clicking as they shifted the ivory rectangles on the bare wooden surface of their table.

With her elbows resting on the counter, Babette was gazing sleepily into the middle distance. After one group of cardplayers had finished, she glanced up at the wall clock; it depended now on the other group when she could get away. Their game might end at any moment or it might last till midnight.

Not until they left could she start cleaning up for the night, stacking the chairs and putting up the shutters.

The superintendent was the next to leave, after a polite good night to Charles, on whom he bestowed a friendly smile—not at all as if he were the brother of a man whom he had arrested for murder.

At last Babette could have a word with Charles. "What have you been doing? I haven't seen you all day."

"I'll tell you later." He shot a warning glance in the direction of Paumelle, who was watching the cardplayers and commenting in a superior way on the game.

"I understand."

She seemed worn out; but, of course, at the best of times she never looked quite fit.

"Feeling sick?"

"No. It's only my back. It was my day for cleaning the windows."

87

There were many of them, and she had spent several hours on a stepladder, straining her arms to their utmost, not to mention that she had to keep bringing pails of water from the kitchen.

And suddenly, for no reason he knew, a vast sense of discouragement—more than discouragement; despair—came over Charles. Perhaps the superintendent's pills were indirectly to blame. Because now he remembered that he hadn't taken his medicine for twenty-four hours, which meant that he would cough all night.

Aunt Lou, who seemed the picture of health, was about to undergo her third stomach operation, and her husband, the pastry maker, suffered from a strangulated hernia, which depressed him and made him so peevish that people hesitated to talk to him.

Was it like this with every family? What with illness and troubles of all kinds, was life a vale of tears for almost everybody? Even Monsieur Pessart had his worries; it was rumored that for the last three years he had been staving off bankruptcy from month to month, and he certainly had a harassed air and rarely smiled.

Abruptly he said to Babette, without knowing why the idea had crossed his mind: "It's too bad we aren't married yet. It would be so much better if . . . if . . ."

One of his fellow workers at the station had got married two months ago, and for weeks he had been coming to work loaded down with catalogues of furniture and domestic appliances. And you couldn't meet him in the street without his insisting on taking you out of your way to contemplate the little apartment he had rented on the second floor of a new red-brick building.

"Don't worry, Charles. It'll come out all right." But she sighed as she spoke; then moved away when the domino players beckoned to her, wanting to settle for their drinks.

She put the money in the till, dropping her tip into the small can kept for this purpose.

"Going already?"

It was only eleven, and the card game was still in full swing. But Paumelle had risen to his feet and was calling to Babette.

"How much do I owe you, my pet?"

When he had left, Charles whispered in her ear: "I may be back presently."

He couldn't have explained why he had resolved to follow Paumelle instead of taking advantage of the chance he would soon have to kiss Babette for the first time that evening. At any moment now she would be going out into the dark street to put up the shutters. All he knew was that he was in an obstinate mood; that he was feeling almost desperate and had ceased to believe in anything whatsoever—except the sheer malignancy of fate, the helplessness of poor humanity.

In this mood he wouldn't have cared at all if Paumelle had swung around to fight. To be laid sprawling in the gutter would be almost a relief after the tension of the last few hours.

But Paumelle did not look back. After following the waterfront he turned off toward the jetty. There were no houses there, only work yards and sheds, and at first Charles wondered what he was after. Could Paumelle have lured him here to kill him?

No. Paumelle stopped beside a gate in some wooden palings and took a key from his pocket. After closing the gate, he crossed a patch of wasteland, entered a wooden shanty, and lighted a candle.

So that explained it! Charles had often wondered where Paumelle spent his nights now that his father's boat had been allowed to rot away in a nook of the Old Harbor and, what with the rats, was, except for tough nuts like the Twister, unfit for human habitation.

After a long look at the shanty, where Paumelle evidently now lived, Charles noticed a big white signboard glimmering in the darkness. On it was inscribed:

He might easily have thought no more about it and hurried back to the Amiral in time to kiss Babette. . . .

At Monsieur Laroche's house in Rouen, they were still talking about the *Télémaque* and recalling similar tragedies of the sea. Maître Abeille was in the foyer of the theater, eagerly imparting information about the queer ways of the Canut family and the wrist wound that seemed to be the cause of old Février's murder. And Superintendent Gentil was taking off his shoes in his bedroom in the Hôtel de Normandie, near the station.

All was silence where Charles stood, alone in the wet darkness, except for the low sound of waves lapping the waterfront. And suddenly he found himself, almost unconsciously, linking together a number of isolated facts that no one, so far, had thought of trying to associate.

Clovis Robin, the contractor, was Emile Février's brother-in-law; he was the brother of that woman, Georgette Robin, whom Février had met in South America, where she worked for a Chilean family. It was known that they had separated, but this was all; Georgette had never shown up again in her hometown.

And now Charles had discovered that Paumelle had the key to Robin's yard and had been provided with a place in it in which to sleep. Then there was this other fact: that Paumelle was very friendly with Emma, whose café was near the Villa des Mouettes. It was the only place in that part of the town where the lights might well stay on till midnight and where Février might have been a frequent visitor.

There was no question of working out right away what connection, if any, lay between these facts. Nevertheless, Charles had a feeling that he was on the track of something, almost a thrill of discovery. He hurried—it was all he could do not to break into a run—back to the Amiral.

Babette was just putting up the shutters when he arrived.

He grabbed her from behind, swung her around, and pressed his lips to hers, shutting his eyes. So fierce was his embrace that she gave a little cry of pain. After a moment she gently freed herself.

"What on earth's come over you?"

"Oh . . . nothing. Only, I think I'm on to something."

"What? Do tell me."

"Not yet. It's mostly guesswork. But—look! Suppose I come around tonight?"

That was his secret, the only one he hadn't shared with his brother. Twice, but only twice, after the café closed, Babette had opened the small back door and let him in. By that time everyone had gone to bed and she was in her nightdress. He had tiptoed up to her attic room, which was just over Jules's bedroom.

"You understand, don't you? I'll try to explain my ideas. And there's something, too, I want to ask you."

She glanced around nervously to make sure no one was listening. From where she stood, she could see the card-players, who were now adding up the score.

"Do you think it's safe?" she whispered.

"Well, anyhow, I assure you that, as things are, it's most important."

Important not only to talk to her, not only to ask her advice, but also to keep up the mood of feverish elation that his discovery had induced.

"All right. But you'll have to wait a good half hour. And mind you take off your shoes."

Inside the café, Jules rose with an effort.

"You may call that good play; I don't. With king and jack in the same hand, you should have . . ."

A fine rain was beginning to fall.

# 6

THOUGH SHE had been in bed for barely a quarter of an hour, there was already a faint, warm odor of her presence in the air. For it was a tiny attic room, with just space for an iron bed, a washstand, and a curtained recess where Babette's clothes, including the underclothes she had just taken off, hung on three wooden pegs.

With a slight shiver she got back in bed, pulling the blankets up to her chin, while her eyes, shot with golden glints, remained fixed on Charles, whose head all but touched the sloping ceiling.

"Coming to bed?" She spoke in a whisper, because of Jules, who was in the bedroom immediately below.

He hesitated. The light had been on when he entered Babette's room, and he'd glimpsed the slim body under the flimsy nightdress. Also, that special perfume in the air had set his senses tingling. For a moment he had an impulse to throw discretion to the winds, undress, and squeeze into the narrow little bed—as, in fact, he'd done on the two previous occasions.

Then, "No," he murmured, frowning, and sat down on the edge of the bed, lowering himself gingerly so as not to make it creak. "I must have a talk with you, Babette."

Secretly she was rather relieved. She had no great taste for love-making—or hadn't yet acquired the taste. Charles had no idea of this; he'd never troubled his head about it. Actually, he himself had felt rather embarrassed on those two former occasions; somehow it would have seemed more natural for him to resort to a woman like Emma when he felt inclined that way.

Putting his hand under the blanket, he found Babette's hand and fondled it as he spoke.

"I want to tell you what I've done today, and just how far I've got. . . . Perhaps you can help me."

A flurry of wind rattled the dark skylight above their heads.

"We'd better put out the light," Babette said.

Leaning forward, he pressed the switch down.

"Come closer. Mustn't talk too loud."

He could feel Babette's curls tickling his cheek. Then he was conscious of a less agreeable sensation: perspiration was forming in the hollow of his back.

"Well, to begin at the beginning, I met Paumelle . . ."

He spoke slowly, choosing his words. He wanted, above all, to put his thoughts in order; he had a feeling that if he told his story, omitting nothing, this would clarify certain ideas hovering in the back of his mind.

That perspiration was a sign that he was in for one of those bouts of fever he often had at night. His cheeks were growing flushed, his hands clammy, as Babette noticed—but she didn't dare to refer to it. He had stretched himself, fully dressed, beside her, under the sheet, and because of his weight he kept rolling almost on top of her. Sometimes, indeed, she was so ill at ease that she stopped listening; her one thought was to extricate her aching shoulder from the pressure of his arm.

"So, when I saw him staying so long with that Flemish woman, it struck me . . ."

It was the first chance he had had to describe the day's activities, and he found that, clothed in words, they acquired not only more significance, but also a touch of heroism.

"Do move away, Charles. You're hurting me."

"Sorry . . . Of course, the really important thing I've discovered is where he sleeps at night. You see why, don't you?"

She gave his hand a warning squeeze, but he failed to understand, and she whispered: "Ssh!"

They both listened. There were faint creaks on the staircase, as if someone were coming up as quietly as possible.

"Jules?" Charles breathed.

She moved her head, but it was too dark for him to see if she had shaken it or nodded.

"Who's there?" The voice came from the landing outside the door. There was a brief silence. "Now then, Babette! I've caught you good and proper. Who's in there with you?"

"What's the matter?" She tried to make her voice sound as if she'd just waked from sleep.

Unfortunately, the door was neither locked nor bolted. Jules stepped quickly in, switched on the light before Charles had time to wriggle out of the bed.

Jules was in a nightshirt, its lower part hidden by the trousers he had scrambled into before starting up the stairs. His eyes seemed bigger than usual and the lids puffier.

"Ah, so it was you," he remarked, gazing at Charles, without much surprise.

What surprised him was that the young man was fully dressed; his coat was even buttoned. And had Charles sworn he'd never touched Babette, Jules would quite likely have replied: "I wouldn't put it past you!"

Meanwhile, both men were equally embarrassed. Babette had pulled the sheet over her, but Charles was on his feet, and since he and Jules were both of ample stature, neither could move much in the tiny room.

"It ain't the thing to do," Jules grumbled—he sounded more aggrieved than angry—"sneaking in like that when I'm asleep. If you want it that badly, do it somewhere else; I won't have goings-on like that, not under my roof."

"But we're engaged," Charles pointed out.

"All the more reason . . ."

"Listen! It isn't what you think. I had to have a talk with Babette, and you know quite well I never get a chance in the daytime."

"A talk, eh? What about? Look here, you'd better come downstairs with me. . . . Good night, Babette. And don't let me catch you doing this sort of thing again."

He shepherded Charles out, shut the door, and switched the staircase light on. On the floor below, the door of his room stood open, and he paused for a moment, evidently of half a mind to ask Charles in. Then he thought better of it and, followed by Charles, trudged down the next flight of steps to the café, where he turned on one light only. This made the room look quite different, all the perspectives changed.

"Really, you should understand I can't allow such doings on my premises. People would be sure to get wind of it, and it would give the place a bad name."

The stove was still warm, and Jules drew a chair up to it. He did not seem to want Charles to leave—perhaps because he felt one of his attacks of insomnia coming on. As for Charles, he found himself unprepared. Though he had nothing against Jules, he never felt easy with him. The reason may have been that, for Aunt Lou and all his family, the landlord of an inn or bistro was a somewhat reprehensible person, a dubious link between respectable people and reprobates.

To make things worse, Jules was notoriously foul-mouthed; indeed, he seemed to take pleasure in coarse expressions, which always made Charles wince. And, finally, Jules was getting on for sixty; and Charles belonged to another generation.

"Sit down. After all, it's just as well you came, perhaps."

Censorious people disapproved of Jules because he had once been in jail; but it was for an offense that, paradoxically enough, his customers regarded leniently, that of selling doctored drinks.

"Bring your chair up. I don't want to have to shout. I've a pretty good idea what you were telling the girl about just now; I've had my eye on you all evening."

Charles had meant to keep his discoveries to himself, but he had little doubt that Jules would worm them out of him if he applied himself to it. With Jules, he always felt like a small boy in front of his teacher.

Just then he had a fit of coughing, and Jules said severely: "You silly young fool!"

"Sorry! I must have got too hot and . . ."

"No wonder, getting into bed fully dressed like that. Didn't you hear what I said? Bring your chair closer to the stove. . . . Wait. Get the third bottle from the right, on the second shelf, and a couple of glasses."

"Thanks, but I don't . . ."

"Do as I told you. A drink is what you need." Jules kept silent for a moment; his look conveyed that he had something on his mind and couldn't decide whether to speak or not. Then, fixing his eyes on Charles, he said: "Paumelle told us you'd been following him all day."

"Not all day. Only this afternoon."

"So you think he did it?"

Charles wondered what to reply. Of course, it wasn't the same here as in the magistrate's office. He had half a mind to confide in Jules. But he needed more encouragement. So he temporized.

"Well, I wouldn't say that."

"But you think it. . . . Put that bottle back on the

counter. Sit down. I hate talking to people when they're standing. Apparently, you're sure it wasn't your brother who did the old man in, aren't you?"

"Of course I am. And so is everybody else who knows him."

"Maybe. I won't deny that. But . . ."

"But what?"

"No, that can wait. You've got it into your head that it might have been Paumelle because he's a young scallawag anyhow. Ain't that so?"

"Well, I saw him at Emma's place."

"What of that?"

"It's quite near Février's house."

"That don't prove anything."

"It might. Likely as not, Emma's place was still open at midnight—on the night Février was killed."

This seemed to impress Jules, who kept quiet for a while, and Charles wondered if he shouldn't produce his final argument. But just when he was about to speak, Jules drew a deep breath and leaned back in his chair, like a man who has at last decided to come out with what he knows.

"There's no telling, of course, how things will turn out. Your brother's a good man, and it's real tough luck he should be in jail if he's not done anything. But I think you're barking up the wrong tree, if you want to fix it on Paumelle."

The tone in which he spoke conveyed that he didn't share Charles's aversion for the young man.

"He's a loafer, I agree, but that ain't his fault—not altogether, anyhow. If you and your brother hadn't had your aunt to look after you . . ."

Charles made an impatient gesture. It looked as if the man was trying to discourage him by proving that his suspicions were unfounded and he'd wasted his day's work.

"Mind you, I'm not defending him. If he bumped off old

Fevrier, the sooner they arrest him the better, and if they pin it on him, he's sure to get it in the neck, considering the sort of reputation he has."

The shutters were still drawn, and, with its single light, the café looked like a stage after the show is over. Charles could picture Babette lying awake upstairs, straining her ears to catch every sound; it must surprise her that her employer hadn't gone back to his room.

"You're too young to know about . . . about some things that I know. Anyhow, I don't mind telling you about them, for what they're worth. Then you can do what you like about it. It's your business, not mine. You never came across Georgette Robin, did you?"

"No."

"Well, I knew her when she was a chambermaid in a hotel and her brother worked in a mason's yard. . . . Now, listen well to what I'm saying; it may have more importance than you think. . . . Georgette was a real juicy bit in those days, the prettiest girl in Fécamp; this kid Babette you're soft on ain't a patch on her, for looks. . . . No, don't get angry. That would get you nowhere, and you'd be sorry tomorrow morning. You got to let me tell it in my own way, and I ain't one to mince my words. . . . Go to bed with Babette as often as you like, but not in my premises. And if you want to marry her, please yourself. I daresay you'll regret it someday. I was like you. I wanted to marry Georgette; in fact, we'd fixed it up between us. Only . . ."

Charles gazed with wide-eyed amazement at the man sitting in front of him. He'd never dreamed that romance —if you could call it that—had played a part in the hard-bitten café owner's life. And once again he realized that until now his interests had been so centered on himself and his family that he'd been blind to all that went on around him; he'd never even tried to understand how others lived and what they thought.

After all, it was only natural that the men of the previous generation also should have had their love affairs; that once upon a time Jules had had a "Babette" of his own—whose name was Georgette. He fell to wondering if Jules had sometimes gone to her room at night. And the next thing Jules said was:

"I did like you. I took off my shoes before going up the stairs; but once I was in her room, I took off more than that. Of course, as I told you, she was quite different from that silly child you're stuck on. She was hot stuff, was Mademoiselle Georgette. I was a waiter at the time, if you want to know; I worked at the station buffet. One day Georgette's brother said he'd bash my face in if I didn't leave his sister alone, and a fine old fight we had, he and I, just outside the station. He gave me a black eye, but I flattened his nose out good and proper. Then, about a week after, Georgette took up with another fellow, and six months later she sailed for South America with a family who'd come to Etretat for the summer. . . . Your dad was doing his military service at the time, if I remember right."

Charles had a feeling all this was leading up to something, some sensational revelation, maybe, and he was impatient for Jules to get on with his reminiscences.

"In those days I knew Février to talk to. He sometimes came to the buffet for a drink. But I never guessed that one day he'd end up in South America and marry Georgette, and they'd live together for years and years. . . . Well, my boy, I can tell you're beginning to see what I'm driving at. But I ain't finished yet."

Just then Charles had a glimpse of a shadowy form in the doorway. It was Babette, who had slipped her dark-green coat over her nightdress and was gazing at the two men with startled eyes. Charles's look betrayed him.

Jules swung around and shouted at her gruffly:

"Go back to bed, damn it! At once. We're having a little talk, and we don't want you butting in." His eyes fell on her feet. "You little fool! You haven't even put your slippers on. Do you want to catch your death of cold? Now then, will you go, or do I have to get up and shove you up the stairs?"

Reassured, she turned and vanished up the staircase.

"Did you ever see the like? Walking about barefoot on a winter night, when she's none too fit as it is! But these youngsters nowadays, that's how they are—not an ounce of sense. . . . Now then, what was I saying? . . . Really, I wonder why I'm telling you all this. Oh, well, now I've started . . . Georgette and Février got sick of each other—I don't know why and I don't care. They separated, got divorced maybe, but I never heard for sure. But there's one thing I do know, and it'll make you sit up. On February second, someone saw Georgette at Havre, and there was a man with her. Perhaps she's got married again, or it may have been just a boy friend."

Charles opened his mouth, but was too dumbfounded to get a word out. This last revelation and all the possibilities it opened out had staggered him.

"She's still there, at Havre. Someone saw her there yesterday. That time her brother was with her, in a café on the Place Gambetta."

The more valuable his information became, the surlier his voice grew. It was as if he were thinking: I'm a fool to take all this trouble over you, my boy. Still, now I've started, I may as well go on. This is what I know, and it's for you to make what you can of it.

Meanwhile, Charles was pondering deeply, linking what he had just heard with the facts he had discovered for himself: the nearness of Emma's *estaminet* to Février's house, Paumelle's intimacy with Emma and his use of Clovis Robin's shed to sleep in. And Clovis's sister had been Février's wife.

He rose abruptly, putting on his cap, as if he intended to dash out into the darkness without waiting to hear more. Jules grinned.

"Hey! What are you up to? . . . Since you're on your feet, bring me that bottle. . . . Of course, it's no use asking you not to let anyone know who told you about Georgette's being at Havre; you'll never have the sense to keep your trap shut."

"I swear to you . . ."

"Don't waste your breath. Have another drink instead. Yes, yes; it's what you need. . . . Now, I'll bet you're going to take the first train to Havre. Ain't that so?"

"Well . . ."

"All very well and good, but how're you going to find them in a big town like that? You'll try all the hotels, eh? Well, for one thing, do you think the hotel people will answer your questions that easy? And if they do, how can you be sure that Georgette hasn't married again and changed her name?"

"Yes, that's so."

"If you hadn't been in such a damned hurry, I'd have told you where she's staying. It's the Hôtel des Deux Couronnes. So now you know. . . . Good hunting!"

He laughed, but his laugh quickly changed to a wry grimace. One of what he called his "cramps" had gripped him; they began in the center of his chest and spread to his left arm, and he could neither sit nor stand, but stayed doubled up as long as they lasted. Usually on such occasions he staggered to a door and hid behind it.

"What's wrong?"

He signed to Charles not to talk, and waited, knowing from experience that it would go away in a minute or two. At last he straightened his back, smiling wanly.

"It's nothing, really. . . . Off you go! That was a lucky idea of yours, coming to see Babette tonight; or quite likely I'd never have bothered to tell you all this." He drew some deep breaths, shook himself, and, hitching up his trousers, shuffled to the door.

"Well? Why don't you go?" He had drawn back the bolt and was holding the door ajar.

"Oh . . . I . . . I wanted . . ." Charles was too flustered to get it out, but what he wanted was to thank Jules, and also to tell him how sorry he was for him—because the doctor had confided in Charles that poor old Jules was in a pretty bad way. Tonight, he felt especially sympathetic, after what Jules had told him about his having been a café waiter and visiting Georgette in her bedroom.

"Mind you, there may be nothing in it. But, anyhow, you've got something to work on. . . . Good night."

The wet night air hovered around them while, for the first time, Charles shook the café owner's big soft hand. Then, as the door closed behind him, he started off at a brisk pace. . . .

IT WAS disgusting. They wouldn't leave him in peace to digest the facts he had amassed. He had tried to get to his room unheard, had avoided treading on the step that creaked, and had used his pocket flashlight so as not to wake his mother by turning on the landing light.

But no sooner was he on the landing than a door opened. Her eyes blurred with sleep, her hair straggling in wisps over her shoulders, his cousin Berthe—who, knowing she'd have to sleep on the sofa, had put on her oldest dress—came out to meet him.

"Why are you so late?"

Her breath had the stale smell of someone who has slept badly.

"Is Mother all right?"

"Well, she was very restless all day, and her temperature went up a bit in the evening. But, I'm glad to say, she's asleep now."

After a moment she murmured, half to herself: "Where did I put it, now?"

"What?"

"That letter. Wait."

After fumbling in the neck of her blouse she produced a crumpled sheet of yellowish paper. Berthe was plump and had a pink-and-white complexion, now shining with perspiration. Drawn back in a bun, her hair disclosed a high, overprominent forehead. They spoke in whispers, as he and Babette had done.

"It came this afternoon."

It was an official form, partly printed, partly written in ink, and proved to be a notice to Madame Canut that the examining magistrate would be coming to her house to question her at 10:00 A.M. on the following day.

"What do you think?" Berthe asked nervously. "Mama suggested we should ask the doctor to give us a certificate that your mother's too ill to be questioned."

More complications! And just at a moment when he needed to keep a clear head and be left in peace to think things out.

"There's another letter—from the railway."

It was to say that his vacation had been granted, but for four days only, because a member of the office staff had fallen ill.

"Bad news?"

"No," Charles replied absently. "It's all right, really . . ."

It was two in the morning; no sound came from the sleepbound town except a distant murmur of the sea. But neither of them felt like sleeping, though they had nothing much to say to each other and had to control their voices all the time.

"What have you been up to all day?"

"It would take too long to tell."

"Do you know, Charles, Mama's quite worried about you. She's afraid you may do something rash. She says you're a bundle of nerves; and, anyhow, you ought to go about it in a different way."

"What way?" There was a rough edge to his voice.

"Oh, I don't know. But I can't help thinking you should go to see the police and try to explain. If Pierre didn't do it, there should be . . ."

He looked away. For the first time he realized that even in his family they weren't quite sure of his brother's innocence.

"Should be what?"

"You know what I mean," she answered irritably, drawing her shawl more tightly around her chest. "Inquiries made. I don't know how they do such things, but . . ."

She was getting on his nerves. Her mother would have liked her to marry him, Charles; whereas Berthe, he knew, had been in love with Pierre ever since she was quite little. And now he pictured her attending every service at the parish church to pray for Pierre, and making vows on his behalf, likely as not.

"You'd better try to sleep now," he said, glancing toward the door.

"Don't you think I could go home?"

"No. There's no point in going out at this hour of the night. And it's raining; you'd get soaked through."

It was better that she stay, to look after his mother if the need arose; he didn't feel up to it now.

"You don't look like yourself, Charles. Are you ill?"

"No. But I'd rather be alone, if you don't mind."

His original intention had been to leave for Le Havre by the early train, at six-twelve. But the letter Berthe had shown him made him hesitate. Might it not be wiser to be at home when the magistrate called?

He could picture the upheaval in the little house when the magistrate turned up, accompanied by his clerk and probably by that damned squirt of a lawyer, too! They'd be certain to start poking and prying; his mother would be frightened, and have one of her attacks, likely as not. He could even visualize the crowd gathering in the narrow street to see what could be seen.

Then a picture rose before him of Pierre in his jail cell, and it gave him a twinge of physical pain so intense that he grimaced.

"Now please go back to bed, Berthe. I'm going to try to get some sleep."

But he couldn't decide if he'd better sleep or go on thinking. He had completely lost his bearings—that was the truth of it—and though he had a definite feeling that events were moving swiftly, heading to a climax, it seemed impossible to get the facts into perspective or see what they pointed to. . . . At last Berthe made a move.

"Good night, Charles."

They kissed each other on the cheek as usual, and Berthe crept back through the darkness to the sofa on which she had been sleeping in the room adjoining Madame Canut's. Charles listened for a moment. He could hear his mother's breathing, and it sounded regular.

"No, I won't tell them anything," he decided, as he began to undress.

The act of undressing recalled to him Babette's room, and he vaguely regretted having failed to take advantage of the opportunity there. Now, however, it vexed him to know that years ago Jules had been doing exactly the same thing, going by night to visit a young chambermaid in a hotel bedroom. Somehow it cheapened Babette. Poor little Babette, she was another who had no luck; always ailing—as the café owner had reminded him. . . . And Jules hadn't married his Georgette after all.

Would it be that he, too . . . ?

He couldn't get to sleep. The bed was stone-cold; his feet felt frozen. Probably he would start coughing and keep it up all night.

Obviously, the simplest course would be, as his cousin had suggested, to tell all he knew to the magistrate or, preferably, to the superintendent, who would perhaps understand better. Then they'd start inquiries at Havre and possibly discover the truth about old Février's death.

But then a memory flashed back of Pierre, as he had seen him last, in the magistrate's office, disdaining to protest or answer his accusers. No, it was out of the question. He and he only could save Pierre, and save him he must, at any cost.

He kept changing his position in bed, and each time he did, it lost a little of its warmth.

105

The truth was, no one had ever given him a helping hand. He had been born under an unlucky star. Most people when they were little had a father and a mother to look after them, and when they did something silly or got into trouble, it didn't matter so much; their parents got them through it.

But he had never had anyone to lean on. When he was a small child he was always being told to be a man. "Your poor dear mother needs your help; it's your duty to look after her." Of the two, his mother was the one more like a child. And his Aunt Lou would add: "You're more intelligent than your brother, Charles, so you must do the thinking for the pair of you."

He had acted as they wished and played the man from his earliest years. With the result that he had never had a real boyhood, never been twelve or fifteen or eighteen; and it was a fact that now, at the age of thirty-three, he was having his first real love affair.

Perhaps at last—or was it too much to hope for?—a day would come when he would hear someone say gently, understandingly: "You needn't worry any more. Take things as easy as you like. I'm here to look after you."

A day would come, perhaps. . . . But at present they were, as usual, shifting the responsibility to his shoulders. They even stayed up at night in order to show him, the moment he got home, dog tired, a message from that wretched magistrate. And, of course, expected him to decide what was to be done about it.

What about Jules? Jules was almost the first person who had spoken to him rather as one talks to a child, gruffly perhaps, yet kindly, almost protectively. Nonetheless Jules had wound up by saying, or as good as saying: "Well, that's all I have to tell. The rest is up to you, and you'd better get a move on."

He was tired as one is tired after heavy physical exertion, when every bone and sinew aches in a different way. Yet he couldn't get to sleep. Though he tried to dispel it, a picture of Georgette kept forming before his eyes. He had never seen her, but he visualized her as rather like Babette, but plumper and older—a cross between Babette and Emma. And, though he had absolutely nothing to go on, he even pictured her companion as a well-built man with a big brown mustache.

What could they be up to in Havre, the pair of them, and why should Clovis Robin (whom nobody at Fécamp liked) have gone to join them? Suppose he told the super-intendent . . . ?

At that moment he felt like weeping, but just then he fell into a heavy sleep, from which he was awakened by a voice in his ears: "Hurry up, Charles. The car's come."

What car? It was broad daylight. From the street came the usual morning sounds. Aunt Lou had put on her black silk dress and had her gold locket dangling from her neck as if she were dressed for a wedding or a public function.

"Listen! That was a ring. I'll go down and let them in."

He peered from the window as she went downstairs. The first person he saw was his pet aversion, Maître Abeille. Monsieur Laroche, the magistrate, in a light over-coat, looked less portentous.

He glanced around hastily. His door had just opened, and he saw his mother on the threshold. She, too, was dressed as if for some ceremony, her hair was carefully done, and she had the expression she always wore when not suffering from an attack, the expression of a rather forlorn, docile little girl.

She, too, said, "Hurry up," and added: "I'm certain now that they're going to release Pierre. Put on your best suit. Aunt Lou is showing them into the living room."

Voice and manner were composed, but it was precisely when she was like this that she was most alarming.

# 7

A DISTANT observer might have taken it for a funeral. Two policemen were posted outside the Canuts' house and near them was a noisy squad of reporters and press photographers. Keeping discreetly in the background were isolated groups of townspeople, like those who stand waiting for a funeral procession to form and then follow it on foot as far as the church.

The cobblestones were wet and glistening, but the rain had stopped; indeed, a half-hearted sunbeam was toying with the big colored poster on a fence opposite the house.

Some neighbors entered Madame Lachaume's pastry shop, ostensibly to buy cakes or rolls, but actually to glean what news they could. Unfortunately for them, only old Lachaume was serving at the counter, and he was rather deaf.

"Don't fidget like that, Charles. My nerves are bad enough as it is."

They were in the ground-floor kitchen, where no one ever went, and there was no fire. The magistrate had forbidden Charles to enter the living room with his mother, saying to him rather curtly: "I'll see you presently."

Aunt Lou had done her best. "Can't I come in, too?

Really, there should be someone with her, in case . . ."

"If we need you, we'll call you in."

So Charles and his aunt had retreated to the kitchen. Its glass door was screened with a light net curtain, and they kept their eyes fixed on it, waiting to see the living-room door, which faced it, open.

"Why, Charles, you haven't even drunk your coffee!"

That was so. Though he had slept much later than usual, he didn't feel any the better for it—not even up to drinking a cup of café au lait. Sitting on a corner of the table, he was staring listlessly in front of him. Now and again his aunt would heave a loud sigh, like a mourner in a death chamber waiting for the undertaker's men to come. The house was no longer theirs; it seemed utterly different from the home they knew.

Once, the living-room door opened, and the magistrate's clerk appeared, fountain pen in hand, and asked Charles politely: "Have you by any chance a bottle of ink?"

With the door open, they could hear the magistrate talking away, but they could not catch what he was saying.

"Will he be much longer?" Aunt Lou asked anxiously.

"No, I don't think so."

Altogether, it lasted three-quarters of an hour, and by then the sun was level with the small window above the front door and was lighting up the imitation-marble wallpaper in the hall.

At last the door opened again, and this time it was the magistrate who came forward.

"Madame Lachaume!"

"Come, Louise," said Madame Canut. "Tell them it's quite true—that I've been saying that it was I who killed Février. For some reason they won't believe me, and . . ."

Charles gave a start, and slipped off the table to his feet. It so happened that these words of his mother had crystallized a thought that, vague as yet and incoherent, had been hovering in the back of his mind. A moment before he heard them he had reached no decision, but now he walked firmly across the hall to the living-room door. Aunt Lou was holding his mother's arm and shepherding her out.

"Ah, there you are, Charles. Tell them."

Tell them what? What did she want of him? Probably to confirm her statement that she was the murderer. But in Charles's mind the words had taken on a different meaning.

"Well? Is it my turn?" His voice was gruff, and he cast his eyes gloomily around the little room.

"Yes. Come in."

"Think of Pierre, Charles," his mother whispered over her shoulder.

There was no need to remind him to do that. As he walked across the linoleum, he saw some ashes from Maître Abeille's cigarette on it. The clerk had cleared the table of the ornaments that usually stood there and had spread out his papers on it. The magistrate, who had taken off his coat, was seated directly under the portrait of Charles's father.

"Is your mother often taken like that?" he asked as soon as the door was closed.

Obviously the interview with Madame Canut had left a strong impression on his mind, and Charles glanced around the room as though expecting to discover some trace of what had happened.

"At first," the magistrate continued, "she was quite composed and reasonable. But after a while she seemed to lose control of herself, and started telling us to arrest *her*. She declared it was she who'd murdered Février."

The magistrate's manner was much less aloof; indeed, he was looking at Charles in quite a friendly way. It was as if this glimpse of the younger man's home had made him understand things better. Which, perhaps, added to his amazement when he heard Charles assert with the utmost coolness:

"My mother was talking nonsense. It was I who killed him."

Then he went up to the clerk, who was staring hard at him, and, leaning over his shoulder, went on speaking.

"Will you record my statement, please? Thank you . . . First, I must tell you why I wanted that man to leave Fécamp. My mother's attacks were becoming more frequent and more severe, and it was seeing him that caused them. I wrote to him twice, asking him to leave down, but I received no answer. Still, I was determined he should go, and on the night it happened I followed my brother to Monsieur Février's place. I felt pretty sure that Pierre would let the old man talk him around. So when I saw Pierre going away I entered the house."

"How did you enter it?"

"By the front door."

"How did you open it?"

"I rang. Monsieur Février himself came to the door."

"Excuse this interruption," Abeille put in. "But there's one point I'd like cleared up. Which bell did you ring, the one with a knob you have to turn, or the one with a bell-pull?"

"The one with the bellpull."

The lawyer beamed with satisfaction. "It's just too bad, but—there isn't any bell. There's only a knocker."

"I didn't really notice. I had other things to think about." Why must that wretched little lawyer put his oar in? And what was happening upstairs? He could hear people moving in his mother's bedroom.

Charles was all the more resolute because, on waking that morning, he had realized that the plan which, the night before, had seemed so promising had actually little hope of success. Going to Le Havre was easy enough, but once he was there what would his next move be? Obvi-

111

ously to go to the Hôtel des Deux Couronnes. But what then? How could he expect to elicit any useful information from Georgette or the man with her, whoever he might be? They were not bound to answer him, still less to incriminate themselves.

Whereas if he accused himself, they'd have to release Pierre, and, moreover, precious time would be gained. He could engage another lawyer, a man who knew his job, and insist on inquiries being made along the lines he indicated.

It puzzled him why the three men in the room, especially the magistrate's clerk, who looked like a decent sort of fellow, were eying him in such a curious way. What could they know that he didn't know? And why, after glancing at the portrait on the wall, did the magistrate rise, walk slowly up to Charles, and place his hand on his shoulder?

"A few minutes ago," he said, "when your mother accused herself of the crime, I put one question, and one only, to her. In what part of the room was the desk?"

Lowering his eyes, Charles said: "Yes? And what did she answer?"

" 'On the left of the door.' "

Charles gave a harsh laugh.

"Naturally my mother didn't know. She's never been to Février's house."

"And you, who have been there—can you answer that question?"

"Yes. The desk was at the far end."

"The far end of what?"

"Of the living room, obviously."

"In front of the window, you mean?"

"Yes."

All three kept silent, and Charles wondered if he'd guessed right or, like his mother, made a blunder. "Well?" he asked anxiously.

"You're wrong," the magistrate said.

"What do you mean?"

"I mean that the desk stands, and has always stood, midway between the two windows. There are two windows in the room, not one, as you seem to suppose."

Charles seemed to crumple, his shoulders sagged, and he gazed dully at a corner of the table and a patch of linoleum below. He was vaguely conscious that the magistrate was talking to him again, but at first the words were a mere buzzing in his ears that had no meaning. The magistrate repeated his remark.

"What is there about your brother that makes everyone stand up for him like this?"

Silence. Abruptly the words took effect on Charles, and went on echoing in his mind. "What is there about your brother . . . ?"

His eyes roved to the faces of the three men from Rouen, but he saw them indistinctly, like figures seen through a curtain. Something had just dawned on him, something that didn't concern the present moment or this morning's events. It reached much farther back, into a haze of unremembering, and he couldn't have expressed it in words.

The buzzing in his ears had stopped, and now he seemed to hear Aunt Lou's voice. "Never forget, Charles, your brother needs you, and you must do your best to look after him." Often, so often, she used to say such things, even when he was quite a small boy. Why, when they were together anywhere, would people stop to stare at Pierre, and exclaim, "What a nice-looking boy!" Why was it always Pierre they looked at, though the two of them were as much alike in those days as twins can possibly be?

Then there was Berthe, who, though she would have consented to marry him, Charles, was secretly in love with Pierre.

Why had he, Charles, if the truth were told, lived a

reflected life, as it were—one that took its form and color solely from Pierre's life and Pierre's achievements?

Several times he'd noticed Babette casting admiring glances in his brother's direction. And on the previous evening Jules had said, or as good as said: "If I'm giving you a hand, it's for Pierre's sake I'm doing it."

For Pierre! It wasn't altogether clear as yet, but a sort of light was dawning in his mind, illuminating trivial, half-forgotten details. Sitting down, he buried his face in his hands, paying no attention to the others. A voice cut through.

"Now listen, Canut!"

He made a vague gesture to show he was listening; but he could apply only half his mind to what the magistrate said.

"Monsieur Pessart has sent a long letter to the public prosecutor; it is signed by a large number of local ship-owners and fishermen."

Naturally! Monsieur Pessart, too, was championing Pierre. . . . Not that, he Charles, was jealous of his brother; quite the contrary. He was jealous of all those others who could do something to help Pierre in this crisis of his life.

"Though the evidence as it stands would justify my committing this case to the next Assizes, I shall not act precipitately, but continue my inquiries."

Canut held his breath, in order not to speak. It was on the tip of his tongue to say: "Then question Paumelle; and, after him, Georgette and her companion; and then Emma . . ."

But he couldn't make up his mind. He knew that once he'd said this, he himself would play no further part; others would take on the job of saving his brother's life.

"Superintendent Gentil," the magistrate continued, "will remain at Fécamp with an inspector. If you have any information to give, I must ask you to get in touch with him at once."

114

"Can I see Pierre?"

"Not just yet. I am very sorry, but at the present stage of the proceedings, I cannot let you see the prisoner."

Still, the magistrate was very different now from the way he had been in his office in Rouen. The change was in no way due to Charles. It was, rather, the atmosphere of the house that had affected him; simple but eloquent details, like that enlarged photograph of a sailor so much like the twin brothers; the piano in the corner; the oak table with old-fashioned carved legs.

"So you have nothing to tell us?"

Charles shook his head, without meeting their eyes. He felt guilty, yet elated. For now he really hoped to save his brother, and to do it alone, unaided.

The clerk gathered up the papers on the table and placed them in his attaché case. The magistrate put on his overcoat, while Maître Abeille murmured in honeyed tones: "You're much mistaken if you lack confidence in me. No, don't shake your head. I sensed it the first time we met. . . ."

So that was that! The three men walked back to their car, and were promptly mobbed by a group of reporters. Now that it was over, there was again that impression of a funeral. The house was like one from which a corpse has just been carried to a waiting hearse. Never had the living room seemed so empty, the hall so bare and resonant.

"Coming up, Charles?" called his aunt from the landing above.

"Yes . . . just a minute."

He had nothing to say or do upstairs. It wasn't his mother who counted at this moment. What did it matter if she had another attack? Only Pierre mattered now.

Alone, Charles looked up at his father's face and was struck by something about it that had eluded him until now. It wasn't Pierre that his father had been like, though they both were sailors. It was him, Charles, that his father resembled. So much so that Charles felt sure that, had his father lived, he, too, would have had trouble with his lungs.

Looking at the photograph, one could get the impression—like all such fancies, hard to justify—that the face was that of a predestined victim. And perhaps, looking at himself and Pierre, people had a rather similar feeling—that Charles counted for little, and only existed in relation to his brother and the help he could give him.

"Aren't you coming up?"

"Yes, yes. I'm coming." There was a hint of petulance in his voice.

His hand strayed to the piano, and, opening it, he gazed down at the keys, which he hadn't touched for ages. He shrugged his shoulders scornfully. What had possessed him to imagine he had the makings of a pianist? How, indeed, could he ever have done anything solely for himself, or developed independent tastes? Anyhow, his project of learning to play the piano had been stillborn; he had soon lost heart when he realized its difficulties.

And why hadn't he yet married Babette? It wasn't because of his mother, as people thought and Babette herself supposed. No, it was for the usual reason—because of Pierre!

His father was dead, his mother lived in a world of dreams, and he himself was unlikely to make old bones. But what did these things matter, since there was Pierre? Pierre, so handsome and robust, with his proud smile when he scanned the distant horizon; Pierre, whose mere presence thrilled people with confidence and love; Pierre, who had led a full life, without fear or faltering . . .

Slowly Charles climbed the stairs; the door facing him stood ajar. His mother, whom Aunt Lou had put to bed, looked up at him.

"What did they tell you, dear?"

"We'll save him, Mother, I promise you."

She was still looking at him, and he could have sworn there was a shade of reproach in her gaze. Yes, his mother blamed him for being here, at liberty, idling, when Pierre was in jail.

Hurriedly he added: "I did as you did. I told them it was I who'd . . ."

"Yes?"

He was positive of it now; she would have welcomed the substitution!

"But they caught me out, too; I couldn't say where the desk was."

"Do you think you'll discover anything?" his aunt asked in a rather dubious tone. She was tidying up the room and, since the sun had come out again, had opened the window.

"Anyhow, I'm leaving for Havre by the next train."

ONE THING was certain; someone had cut Février's throat, stolen his money and securities, and left the house under cover of darkness. And that "someone" was still at large, read the papers, and knew that Canut was in prison and the inquiry proceeding.

Did that person know also that at this moment Charles was walking the sunlit streets of Le Havre? Or observe him entering the Hôtel des Deux Couronnes, and note that he looked ill at ease, since it was a somewhat luxurious hotel, with marble steps leading up to a spacious lounge, and that he was asking the price of a room?

"With or without a bathroom?"

Without, obviously! He would have liked to examine the registration book, lying on the mahogany desk, but didn't dare to right now.

"Have you any more luggage?"

"No. I won't be staying long."

He had only a small suitcase, containing a single change of clothes. A man with a striped waistcoat led him up to a room overlooking the square. Once the door was closed, he felt completely at a loss.

It was always like that. He would embark on an undertaking full of zeal, but seeing it through was another matter. A man and a woman were talking in the next room, rather loudly; they seemed to be quarreling. Could they be the two he was after? No, that was expecting too much. . . . He went downstairs again.

"Excuse me, madame. There's something I want to ask you."

Placid, framed by two spiky palms, the woman at the desk looked at him and murmured, "Yes?"

"I have an appointment," he continued hastily, "with two friends who are staying here, a gentleman and a lady. I haven't seen them for years. The lady's name is Georgette."

"Is she dark and rather stout?"

"Yes . . . Well, I think so."

"You mean Madame Ferrand, don't you?"

"That's right. Someone came to see her. From Fécamp."

"Her brother, yes. I'm afraid I can't tell you where they are just now."

"Aren't they in the hotel?"

"No, they're out. They're never in their rooms much in the daytime. I wouldn't be surprised if you found them in the Taverne Royale. They told me I could get them there if there was a telephone call."

Like the Deux Couronnes, the Taverne Royale was a more luxurious type of place than those Charles usually patronized. However, he walked boldly in, settled down on a banquette near the window, and ordered a glass of beer.

He felt so much out of his element, so void of thought, that had anyone accosted him just then and asked what he was doing here, in Le Havre, he'd have found it hard to reply.

Yet what he was doing was obvious enough. He'd come to watch some people whom he didn't know, in the hope of finding evidence to prove that these people had robbed and killed old Février.

118

All this had seemed feasible enough in the seclusion of the Café de l'Amiral, even in the queer, conspiratorial atmosphere of Emma's *estaminet*. But here in Le Havre, on a sunny day and in his present surroundings, such a project seemed fantastic to a degree.

The Deux Couronnes was obviously of the three-star category, with carpets in the hallways, running water in the rooms, and brass bedsteads. And the Taverne Royale, too, was a smart place, with big plate-glass windows, chandeliers, and a platform for a band, which would presumably start playing at five o'clock.

How could one possibly imagine that in such a setting . . . ? Just then Charles nearly dropped his glass, and felt like kicking himself. He'd realized that he had clean forgotten the name the woman in the hotel had given him. And he knew he'd never have the nerve to tackle her again about it.

Wait now! It was the name of some town or other, a well-known French town. Châlons? No. It was a bigger place and it ended in *an* or something that sounded like an *an*. Grignand? No, that wasn't it either. But he was getting warm. There was an *F* in it, wasn't there? And somehow it was associated with high mountains.

What a damned fool he was not to have jotted down the name at once! For a good ten minutes Charles wrestled with the problem, then gave it up; his attention had been diverted to some people coming in.

Then "Got it!" he exclaimed. "Ferrand!" He was sure that was the name, and the town he'd had in mind was Clermont-Ferrand.

A man and a woman had just taken the seats facing him, and he let his eyes rest on them for a moment. Suppose it's they? But he didn't really think it.

The woman, very fat and lavishly made up, was dressed much younger than her age, which was, Charles judged, fifty or over. Her companion, a man of thirty-five or forty, had a washed-out complexion and a rather hangdog air.

The chief impression he gave was one of extreme bore-
dom. When the waiter asked what he wanted to drink, he
turned languidly to the woman beside him.

"And you, my dear?"

She ordered café au lait. While he was still hesitating,
his eyes settled on Charles's beer and this seemed to decide him. But at the last moment he changed his mind and
asked for mineral water.

Why shouldn't they be the pair Charles was after? Still,
they did not look like people with a crime on their conscience, merely like people who are bored with things in
general, including each other's company. They did not
speak. The man picked up a newspaper and ran his eyes
over it, while the woman stared out of the window at the
passers-by.

After their drinks had come, the two exchanged some
remarks that Charles failed to catch. Then the man called
the waiter and asked him something. Presently the waiter
came back from the cashier, and, when he shook his head,
Charles had an intuition: They wanted to know if there
had been a phone call for them.

He was used to sitting for hours on end at a café table,
because of Babette. And so, it seemed, were the pair he
was observing; they showed no signs of impatience, didn't
fidget, and merely toyed with their drinks.

The band came in, mounted the platform, and played a
Viennese waltz. Gradually the place filled up, and the
street, too, grew more crowded.

Suppose that woman was Georgette? Charles tried to
picture her as the "real juicy bit" Jules had kept company
with in former days. It wasn't inconceivable; they were
much the same age, and she might have been quite pretty
once.

And someday, perhaps, Babette, too . . . His thoughts
swerved off on a familiar track, "looking for trouble," as
Pierre called it. He had a knack of thinking ahead and
always on the gloomiest lines, anticipating the worst. Yes,

Babette might well develop into a fat old creature like the woman in front of him. But by that time, he, Charles, would have been dead for many, many years. Not so Pierre. Pierre was the staying kind; he would ripen into one of those white-haired old fellows who are universally respected and whose advice is sought by their juniors.

He gave a start. The street door had opened, and a man was coming to the table at which the two were seated. It was Clovis Robin, wearing rubber boots over his shoes, as he did at Fécamp, and a seaman's cap.

Robin shook hands with the woman, then with the man, and sat down in front of them, with his back to Charles. When the waiter came, he rose to take off his coat, with a loud sigh of relief—he was a burly, florid-cheeked man—and while he was doing so, his eyes fell on a face reflected in the mirror opposite. For a moment he stopped moving, one arm still in the coat sleeve, and frowned.

He had recognized Charles. For some seconds he stood staring at Charles's reflection, wondering, it seemed, what had brought him here. And Charles had a faint feeling of physical fear, because the building contractor was twice as strong as he and his bushy eyebrows gave him a formidable air.

But nothing happened. Robin sat down again and started talking to the other two, leaning forward as one does in a crowded café where, making conversation still more difficult, a band is playing.

And now, Charles wondered, was he any farther along? What could he do? Robin had come to Le Havre to see his sister and her husband—or lover. What of that? Could anything be more natural than that they should meet in a café for a friendly talk? It was absurd to find any sinister significance in this.

On seeing Charles, Robin had not displayed the least alarm; only the mild surprise one normally has when unexpectedly running into someone from one's hometown at a considerable distance from it. And if he hadn't wished him good day, that was because Robin knew Charles only by sight; they had never spoken to each other.

Georgette was laughing heartily—why, there was no knowing. Her companion got no farther than a weak grin; his face wasn't the kind that lends itself to laughter. Neither of them had looked in Charles's direction, as they certainly would have had the building contractor made some allusion to him.

"Waiter! Bring me a grenadine-and-bitters."

Some fifty people in the café were talking at the top of their voices, the band was playing fortissimo, and what with the constant tinkle of saucers and glasses, there was no possibility of hearing what Georgette and the others said. Yet even if Charles had overheard, quite likely it would have meant nothing to him.

A maddening situation! So it was only to come to this that he had had that nocturnal talk with Jules in the dimly lit Amiral; only to come to this that he had set out for Le Havre with such high hopes . . .

In his discouragement Charles was half inclined to hurry back to Fécamp. Otherwise Robin would be sure to learn that he was staying at the same hotel as his sister —not at all the sort of hotel Charles would patronize ordinarily; and this would rouse his suspicions.

"Monsieur Ferrand, you're wanted at the phone."

The man got up as anyone does when called to the phone, not at all like a criminal expecting some important news. Unhurrying, he threaded his way between the tables toward a small telephone booth resplendent in polished mahogany.

The brother and sister did not take advantage of his departure to exchange confidences; both remained silent. They waited tranquilly, as one awaits the return of a friend before resuming a conversation interrupted by his departure. In fact, the whole scene was deplorably normal, matter-of-fact. None of them was behaving like a person with something on his conscience.

True, Robin was unpopular in Fécamp, but that was only because he had a reputation of being mean to his workers and overcharging customers. But these were common practices with small-town builders; there was nothing more against him.

And the other two, the woman and the man, were just like so many couples one sees in restaurants and cafés; the woman getting on in years, overdoing the makeup and wearing too much jewelry, and the man, still young, weak-looking, a sort of ineffective gigolo.

When Ferrand returned, his expression was exactly the same as before. He spoke at some length, presumably telling the others his conversation over the phone.

Robin shifted his head slightly and gave a side glance at Charles. Now only, it seemed, did he tell the others about him. Charles almost fancied he could hear the words.

"He's a young fellow from Fécamp, the brother of that man Canut who's in jail."

Georgette gave him a long stare, while Ferrand bestowed on him a languid glance—precisely the kind of glance one bestows on someone whose family has been figuring in the newspapers.

A newsboy was going around the tables. Charles bought a paper and saw on the front page a photograph of his home, with the magistrate and the lawyer standing at the gate, surrounded by reporters. A subhead read: "Mme Canut and her son Charles successively accuse themselves of the crime."

So things that concerned his mother and himself alone, the happenings in the little living room, were being blazoned forth for the callous world to gape at! And they went into details, mentioning his mother's and his own failure to state the correct position of the dead man's desk.

Charles turned to the "Latest News" on the last page. "A Dramatic Development in the Février Murder Case. Dead Man's Will Discovered. Février Bequeaths his Entire Estate to Mme Canut."

He half rose from his seat and all but started pacing up and down the room. Then, glancing at the other table, he saw the same paper lying on it, still folded.

Our readers will remember that M. Février's murderer robbed his victim of a bundle of securities, as well as of a considerable sum of money that was kept in the drawer of his desk.

The fact that no will could be found led the authorities to believe that this, too, had been stolen. However, this afternoon, there was a dramatic discovery; on returning to his office in Rouen, the examining magistrate, M. Laroche, found in his mail an envelope containing the missing will.

No letter was included with it, and the address on the envelope was composed of words cut out of a newspaper.

We are not yet able to state whether this will, in which M. Février bequeaths his whole estate to Mme Canut, is genuine or not. It contains a provision that in the event of the lady's refusing to accept the legacy, it is to go to the Seamen's Benevolent Fund.

It is impossible to judge the bearing of this new development on the inquiry now in progress. Our reporter called at Mme Canut's house this afternoon, but was informed that she was ill in bed and had not yet been told about the will. We hear that Charles Canut, the prisoner's brother, left Fécamp this morning, but it is not known where he has gone.

Looking up, Charles saw Robin fingering a siphon, then nipping off the end of a cigar with his teeth and fumbling for his lighter in his waistcoat pocket. At other tables some ten or twelve people were reading the same paper as Charles had read, while the band played the "Blue Danube."

# 8

"Who's speaking?" She had to ask it several times, and her voice, pitched a tone higher for talking over the phone, had a stridence that brought out its common intonation. "Who's that? I can't hear. . . . Yes, it's me, Babette. Oh, is that you, Charles? Just a moment, while I shut the door."

The telephone was on the wall of the hallway between the main room and the kitchen, and there was a noisy crowd in the former.

"Yes." She was tugging at her apron string, which was too tight around the waist. "Where are you? Still at Havre? Aren't you coming back? . . . Don't put your mouth so near the receiver; I can't hear half you say."

She kept her eyes on the door, which might open at any moment. There were at least ten customers waiting to be served, and Jules was in one of his irritable moods.

"Listen, Charles, you can tell me all that when you're here. I have some news for you. For one thing, the *Centaur's* back. The crew are sick at heart; they had a rotten catch, only two hundred barrels, and the *Saint-Michel* had nearly five hundred."

The trouble was that Charles kept trying to put a word

125

in, and, because he persisted in shouting, his voice made her ear buzz.

"Do please stop talking. I want to tell you something . . . No, I can't speak any louder." Babette was still casting nervous glances toward the door. "Listen! I was told an hour ago that Paumelle has disappeared. . . . Yes, run off. He's left Fécamp for good, they say. That's all. When will you be back? . . . If there's a train? . . . Yes, we'll stay open late tonight—because of the *Centaur* and the *Saint-Michel*. Bye. See you later."

She hung up with a sigh of relief; the telephone always made her nervous. Straightening her apron, she went back to work, picked up the tray of drinks she had prepared a few minutes before, and whispered in Jules's ear as she passed the table at which he was beginning a game of cards: "It was Charles."

"Did you tell him?"

She nodded. She didn't dare lie.

"Well?"

"I think he's coming back this evening. Only, there's no train at the junction, it seems; I don't know how he'll manage."

AFTER ALL, what she'd told him amounted to little. Only that Paumelle had left "for good." But it was enough to make Charles resume his seat with a look of complete bewilderment.

The others hadn't moved from their place in a corner. Robin was bending forward, his hands locked on his knees, and was haranguing the others in a low tone. When Charles came back, he gave him a sharp glance.

Throughout the evening Charles had been growing more and more uneasy, and he felt he was near his breaking point. Yet how could he have acted otherwise? Soon after he had finished reading his paper and while the paper on the other table remained folded, Robin had made a careless gesture, uncovering the headline on the front page.

He began reading placidly enough, now and again making some remark to his sister and the man with her. But when he turned to the "Latest News" on the last page, his expression changed and he read out every word in a low tone. After that he cast a puzzled glance at Charles, as if asking what this meant.

One could see his agitation; at one moment he rose to his feet, but presently sat down again. After some ten minutes of conversation with the others he walked to the telephone booth. For the first time, Georgette was eyeing Charles with undisguised curiosity.

As chance would have it, merely to maintain his dignity, Charles chose this moment to beckon to the waiter and pay for his drinks. Had he not done so just then, the course of events might have been different—because the others had settled for their drinks as soon as they were brought.

Robin came rushing from the telephone booth and promptly hustled his sister and Ferrand into the street. Almost without thinking, Charles followed. When they reached the hotel, Georgette went upstairs; the two men stayed in the lobby.

Robin's gaze shifted to Charles, who was standing just outside the entrance. He shrugged his shoulders carelessly, like someone who feels sure of his superior ability in handling a situation and scorns his opponent. Evidently they were in a hurry, for Georgette came down again almost at once, with a leather attaché case under her arm.

The three set off at a brisk pace toward a quiet district of the town, evidently a residential area. A few minutes' walk brought them to a house with a porte-cochere, and Robin reached up to the big brass knocker on the door.

Once again Charles had followed, urged on by his

vague hope of discovering something. Now he stayed planted on the sidewalk, feeling horribly embarrassed by the scowl, more contemptuous than indignant, that Robin was directing at him from the doorstep. Once the door had closed behind the trio, he went up and studied the brass plate: HUBERT JOLINON, SOLICITOR.

The street was dimly lighted, and during a full hour no more than two or three people went by, though the noises of city traffic were clearly audible only a few hundred yards away.

That hour of waiting did not calm Charles. On the contrary, the more he thought about it, the more convinced he was that things were heading for a crisis. The prompt reaction of those three people to the article in the paper that Robin had read out loud and the fact that they'd been in such a hurry to consult a lawyer seemed to point to some dirty work going on behind the scenes. Quite likely he was running into danger. Well, if Robin attacked him and laid him sprawling in the gutter—it couldn't be helped! If only he had some idea of what was in Georgette's attaché case . . . !

The door opened. Some words were exchanged, and the three of them started back the way they had come, but at a slower pace. Now and then one of them glanced back at Charles, who followed some fifty yards behind.

He wondered what steps he should take if, for instance, they went on board a ship. The obvious thing would be to notify the police and have them prevented from leaving France; but would he dare do this? Or suppose they caught a train? How much money did he have with him? Four hundred francs or so, he reckoned, a sum that wouldn't take him far.

And supposing . . .

Just then they turned into a well-lighted street and a few steps brought them to the hotel. Charles followed them in. While Georgette was exchanging some remarks with the woman at the desk, Robin stared hard at Charles and once again shrugged his shoulders.

A moment later a door was thrown open, and Charles saw a white-walled dining room with ten tables laid for dinner, but no one was there except an elderly man sporting the rosette of the Legion of Honor on his lapel. It was all rather embarrassing; Charles knew that his clothes were not good enough, and the emptiness of the place intimidated him as much as the dignified appearance of the headwaiter.

He chose a corner seat and answered yes to a question he had failed to catch; with the result that he was served with the costlier of the two menus, the one at thirty-five francs.

A half-bottle of wine stood on the table, and almost unconsciously he worked his way through it, while the other three, who were at a neighboring table, conversed in low tones. Robin, who sat facing him, now and then gave him a glance, as if to say: "You're wasting your time, my boy. You'd do better to go straight back home."

And at these moments Charles felt all his courage ebbing away.

"Will you have your coffee in the smoking room?"

He said yes again, because he had just seen the others move into an adjoining room, which was as sober and as empty as the dining room. The old gentleman had preceded them and was reading a magazine with a pink cover.

It was shortly after this that Charles had felt impelled to call Babette. There was no special reason, except that he had an idea he should let her know where he was, in case anything happened to him.

He had had no time to explain this, and naturally enough she had failed to understand. In fact, it was she who had done all the talking, and when he sat down again, he felt more at a loss than ever.

Then something happened that made him give a start,

and he discovered to his shame that he was trembling. Robin had risen abruptly and was walking straight toward him. Instinctively he raised his arm, as if to ward off a blow.

"Can I have a word with you? Come to our table."

Luckily the old gentleman was still in the smoking room. They wouldn't dare do anything in his presence. Like a man in a dream he followed Robin. As he approached, he saw Georgette staring at him curiously, and Ferrand, who was smoking a cigar much too big for him, turned his sallow face in his direction.

"Sit down. Do you know my sister?"

He moved his head—whether he shook it or nodded, he had no clear idea—and heard himself murmuring something that sounded like "Pleased to meet you."

"And this is our friend, Monsieur Ferrand." Robin took a sip from his glass of calvados, and added: "What'll you have?"

"Nothing, thanks. I don't drink alcohol."

"I might have known."

Why did he say that? Or was he merely trying to put off whatever "explanations" were to come? For the first time it struck Charles that Robin might be feeling nearly as embarrassed as he was.

"You've read the paper, of course. So you know what they say about this will?"

"Yes."

"Did you know anything about it before?"

"No. I swear I didn't."

"There's no need to swear. I'm not the examining magistrate, and you're not in court. Now listen. I have no idea what game you're playing or think you're playing. But since you're here, I might as well let you know certain facts. . . ." He cut the end of a cigar and slowly lit it. "You have thought fit to follow us all afternoon, and so you know that we have been to see my sister's lawyer and given him certain documents."

While Robin spoke, Ferrand merely nodded approval now and then. Georgette, however, always interested in men, was staring at this one, who might well be a murderer's brother. The boldness of her look, which was both rude and provocative, made Charles blush.

"Your brother's been arrested," Robin continued; "whether rightly or wrongly is no concern of mine. I don't know him, and your family affairs don't interest me in the least."

As he spoke, Robin became a less menacing figure. In fact, he reminded Charles of Jules; he had something of the same gruff, downright manner. And unconsciously Charles noted his trick of swaying his body as he spoke and sometimes shutting his eyes because of the smoke from his cigar.

"I assume it's not mere coincidence that you're staying at this hotel. And it wasn't just to take the air that you've been following us. At the café, it was a near thing I didn't plug you one in the eye, just to teach you to mind your own business."

Evidently the old gentleman had guessed something and was listening; he was no longer turning the pages of his magazine.

"Now, tell me, what exactly do you know about . . . this business?"

"But . . ."

"I'm only asking what you know, nothing else. I suppose people have told you about my sister; ain't that so? That she'd come to Havre and had called on Février?"

"I didn't know . . ."

"Well, you're going to know. A fortnight ago she came to Havre because I sent for her to come from Alfortville, where she's been living for some years. Now don't think I'm afraid of you and that's why I'm telling you this. I simply want to get things straight, so we don't waste our time, you and me."

Charles was uncomfortable, sitting on a Louis XV chair

with a carved back. Still watching him, Georgette took a cigarette from her case and started smoking it, smearing the stub with red from her lips.

"It will be in the papers tomorrow, because I'm going to tell the magistrate what I'm telling you now. My sister met Février in South America, and they got spliced in Guayaquil. It wasn't long before she discovered that her husband was a bit . . . well, let's say, a bit like your mother is. . . . No, don't get upset; no offense meant. He'd be quite okay for months, then all of a sudden like, he wouldn't say a word to anyone, and sometimes for a fortnight. So my sister thought she'd better come back home, to France, and she asked Février for a divorce. He told her it wasn't worth the trouble, since marriages in Ecuador aren't recognized in France, anyhow. Do you follow me?"

Yes, Charles followed, but belatedly, because each of the man's statements conjured up a picture that hovered in his mind for some moments. It had been the same when Jules was describing his affair with Georgette, and Charles visualized her as a fatter, sprightlier edition of Babette. It puzzled him that one could talk in this matter-of-fact tone about events that had meant so much when they took place to these people whose past lives were being disclosed to him, bit by bit. Georgette's life, for instance; her experiences as a chambermaid in a hotel, then her journey to South America and her marriage to Février, who also, like his mother, had "attacks." And then, little by little, the lapse of time had made her what she was now: a fat, elderly woman dripping with jewelry (was it real or fake?), who had returned to France and set up house with Ferrand in a suburb of Paris.

"Two months ago," Robin continued in the same flat, unemotional voice, "Georgette decided she had better legalize her position. Monsieur Ferrand, I should tell you, is an insurance agent, and has a very comfortable income."

One half expected Ferrand to bow acknowledgment of this tribute; Charles saw a well-pleased smile form on his lips and stay there. Indeed, all three of them, the two men and the woman, had a curious fixity in their attitudes and expressions, as if they were posing for a group portrait.

"When they were living in Alfortville they learned that, owing to a change in the law, her marriage to Février was still valid. Georgette didn't know yet that her husband had returned to France and settled in Fécamp, or that he'd come into a little money and a house there. When I mentioned in a letter that he was living in the Villa des Mouettes, she asked me to look him up, to save her the trouble of coming all that way. Février flatly refused to see me. He was like that, you know—not quite all there.... Of course, it must be upsetting to know one's eaten human flesh."

Charles looked hurriedly away. That last remark had almost turned his stomach. Robin shrugged his shoulders.

"Sorry. I'd forgotten. . . . Anyhow, all that's such ancient history, isn't it? . . . See that old fellow over there? He's listening for all he's worth. He'd do better to go on reading his magazine. . . . Well, you see how things stood. If the marriage was valid, my sister shared half of old Février's windfall. Not that the house is worth much, but it's in a good position, and fifty thousand in gilt-edged went with it. So I wrote to Georgette and told her to put in her claim at once, because I'd heard rumors. . . . You know what I mean? Because of your mother's goings-on— no offense meant—Février had decided to move. A real estate agent told me the villa was for sale."

An hour earlier Charles had been living in an atmosphere of crime and danger, thinking that he was playing the hero. This conversation, on strictly bourgeois lines, about investments, house property and the like, had brought him down to earth. The glamour had departed.

"So that's why Georgette came here with her friend. I advised her to come. There was no point in her going to Fécamp; it would only have given rise to gossip. But one day I took her in my car to Février's place; we went there by the back street. Février treated her like he'd treated me; refused to let her in. So the only thing we could do was consult a lawyer, and I went to see Maître Jolinon, though he's a shark for fees. . . . But before he could get anything started someone killed Février. . . . Note that I say 'someone.' They've arrested your brother, but I'm not saying he did it. . . . Anyhow, that's a job for the police. . . . But now something new has cropped up—a will, by which, they say, the old man left his whole estate to your mother. . . . I may as well tell you right away that our lawyer says the will is void, because it disposed of an estate half of which belonged to Février's wife—my sister, that is. So that's that!"

He relit his cigar and gave Charles a look that said: "So you've been cheated."

Charles wasn't "cheated," because he'd never counted on his mother's getting Février's estate. Nonetheless Robin's revelations had been a shock. They had knocked the bottom out of the theory he had laboriously built up, and he'd have to make another start, from scratch.

He looked so crestfallen that Georgette began to giggle and had to turn her head. Meanwhile, Robin kept his eye on the young man, and his look was like that of a farmer at a fair watching the face of a man, with whom he hopes to strike a bargain, for the first sign of vacillation.

Ferrand was moved to put in a word. "Of course, if Février had agreed to a divorce, there'd have been no need for filing a suit. But now that this complication has arisen and the law is on our side, there's no reason why we shouldn't go ahead."

Charles nodded vaguely. What the man said seemed logical enough. He himself could never tell a lie without blushing, and he never imagined others capable of lying. In fact, he couldn't help believing what he was told. So now he was convinced he'd made a mistake and let his imagination run away with him. Robin was obviously out to fight for his legal rights and his sister's, tooth and nail; but Charles was now convinced it wasn't he who had cut the old man's throat. Nor had Georgette. Nor even Ferrand, unprepossessing as he was.

"I'm sorry," he murmured unthinkingly.

Sorry for what? For having suspected them and dogged their steps? He had no idea; all he knew was that he felt he'd been unfair to them.

"I'm sure," he hastened to add, "that my mother will refuse the legacy."

"She certainly will," Georgette riposted, "if she has any wits at all." It was the only remark she had made that showed any ill feeling.

A long silence followed. No one could think of anything more to say. Robin sucked at his cigar, which was almost out again. The old gentleman, pretending to read, was noisily fluttering the pages of his magazine.

"Waiter, bring me another calvados."

At last Charles rose. "I'd better be getting back to Fécamp," he said.

"Hasn't the last train gone?"

"I don't know. What time is it?"

"Half past eleven. You could get as far as La Bréauté by the express. But you'd have to spend the night there."

Georgette glanced at her brother, who gave one of his habitual shrugs. After a few minutes' rumination, however, he said:

"I can take you there in my car, if you like. Wait for me in the lobby, please. I want to have a word with my friends here."

"But . . ."

"Didn't I say I'd drive you to your place? Or are you afraid of coming with me?"

"Of course not!"

Why did he always let himself be impressed by people like Robin and Jules, people who, when all was said and done, were in no sense his "betters"—perhaps the contrary? And why did he never dare stand up to them and say no when he felt like it?

Murmuring a vague good night, he edged his way out of the room, excused himself to the woman at the desk for not staying overnight, and asked shyly for his bill. Never had he been so sadly conscious of his disabilities. All that talk, especially about South America and Alfortville, had made him realize his rusticity and inexperience. To think that he'd been to Paris only once in his life, and then only for the day! And that he still felt himself blushing when he recalled the way Georgette had looked at him!

He sat down on a wicker chair, then remembered his suitcase, and apologized to the elevator boy for troubling him to take him up to his floor.

When he came down, he found the three of them in the lobby. Robin was wearing a thick black overcoat and a cloth cap.

"Ready?"

Georgette held out her hand.

"Do you really think it wasn't your brother who . . . did it?"

Afterward, when trying to recall what he had answered, he found it had completely slipped his memory. All he remembered was that he had shaken hands with her and then with Ferrand. Robin walked briskly, and in a few minutes they were at a cheap garage in the business district, and the building contractor got his car.

"Get in, will you, while I'm filling it up?"

The streets were as crowded as in the daytime, and bursts of music came from some of the cafés. Once they were outside town, they met the full force of a wind off the sea that roared around the car and made it shake. The moon was up, and clouds of two shades, white and silvery gray, were scudding fast and low across it.

Robin, who smelled of brandy, was still smoking a cigar, while he looked straight in front of him, half asleep, it seemed. After some miles, he remarked: "If anybody saw us now, I bet they'd wonder why I'm giving you a lift home in my car." Some moments later he added: "Anyhow, it shows I've nothing on my conscience."

Charles, who had his eyes fixed on the greenish-yellow spot made by the headlights, began to fidget when the first houses of Fécamp loomed up ahead. Robin spoke again.

"Shall I drop you at your place?"

"No, thanks. I'd rather . . ."

"I understand. Get out wherever you want. Personally, I'm going straight home and to bed. I have a busy day here tomorrow, and I'll have to find time to go to Rouen and see the magistrate."

Charles didn't dare bring up the subject of Paumelle, who had been living in one of Robin's sheds and now was said to have disappeared. They had passed the lock gate and the Café de l'Amiral was on their right.

"Here, please," Charles murmured.

Robin stopped the car and, without taking his hands off the wheel, grunted, "Good night."

So this expedition to Le Havre, on which he had set such high hopes, had ended in fiasco. Entering the Amiral, suitcase in hand, he felt rather foolish, but he went in anyway. The lights were still on, but there was no sign of Babette.

"Isn't Babette here?" he asked Jules.

"She's gone down to the cellar for some cider. . . . Well? What happened?"

One of the *Centaur*'s crew, who lived at Bénouville and wouldn't have had time to get back home to sleep, was snoring, fully dressed, on a banquette. He always slept at the café when the *Centaur* stayed only one night in port. The only other person present was the superintendent, who was sitting facing Jules. Jules beckoned to Charles.

"How did you get back? . . . I suppose I needn't introduce the super?" Why did he wink when he said this? Did he mean that Charles could speak frankly in the police officer's presence, or that he'd better be on his guard? "We were talking about you only a moment ago. I said you wouldn't get back tonight, because you'd missed the last train from La Bréauté. I suppose someone gave you a lift. Who was it?"

"Oh, Robin," he replied uncomfortably.

Babette, on her way back with a jug of cider, gave a start on seeing him.

"What'll you drink?" Jules asked. "Babette, give him a brandy. Yes, yes, it'll do you good. When you came, we were wondering how Georgette was taking that bit of news about the will. Must have been a nasty blow for her."

The superintendent smiled faintly. The two men seemed like old cronies, and Charles felt sure that Jules had told him everything.

"You know that Paumelle's cleared out?" Jules continued.

"Yes. Babette told me over the phone."

The superintendent spoke for the first time since Charles had arrived.

"I doubt if he'll get far. We've broadcast his description."

"You've seen the papers, eh?" For some reason Jules winked again.

"Yes." Charles wondered if his answer shouldn't have been No. He felt all at sea, and threw a questioning glance at Babette, who was leaning with her elbows on the counter, a favorite position of hers when there were no customers to serve or glasses to wash. But Babette's answering glance was noncommittal.

"Anyhow, one thing's certain. We found, under that seat, a piece of the newspaper from which he chopped out the words for the address."

"That was easy enough," the superintendent remarked. "All the papers were mentioning Monsieur Laroche, the examining magistrate at Rouen. He only had to cut out that and stick it on the envelope."

"Say, Charles . . ."

"Yes?"

"Do you know what the super was telling me? That he's now convinced it was Paumelle who did it."

But why did he make that remark with a twinkle in his eye? Charles wondered. Perhaps he'd had a drop too much? That must be it; because he had no conceivable reason to see anything funny in a thing like that.

"Well, I told him straight," Jules continued, "that though Paumelle's a young ne'er-do-well, as we all know, murder isn't up his alley. Only, he won't believe me. What do you think?"

"I don't know."

"Yes, I expected you to say that. You're on the track of something, but you'd rather keep it under your hat. That's what I told our friend here just now. Ain't that so, Super? Didn't I say it wasn't the police who'd spot the murderer, but Charles Canut? Just you wait and see. . . . Another round of drinks, Babette."

There was sawdust on the floor and the room reeked of fish and brine, as it always did when fishing boats had come in.

"Did you see Georgette? Has she kept her looks? I'll bet she's a regular elephant by now."

"Well, she's rather fat."

"And the other, her precious gigolo, what's he like? A good-looker?"

It dawned on Charles that Jules was jealous, and eager to hear something to the disadvantage of Georgette's male companion. And he couldn't repress a laugh. He had drunk three glasses of neat brandy, though he knew this meant a sleepless night. Jules addressed himself to the superintendent.

"She's one of those women who can't do without it. When she's seventy, she'll still be snooping around for somebody to sleep with. That's Georgette, and what I don't know about Georgette ain't worth knowing. . . . I'll bet that her eyes, anyhow, haven't changed much, though she's fifty if she's a day." Something prompted him to turn to Charles, with another wink. "Your brother, now. If she set eyes on a young fellow like that, she'd make a pass at him right off."

The superintendent rapped the table with a coin. Babette came at once.

"How much do I owe you?"

"Nothing," Jules put in quickly. "That round was on the house. . . . By the way, did she say if she'd be coming to Fécamp?"

"I really don't know. . . ."

"Damn it! You might have asked her that."

"Well, she told me she came here once, in Robin's car, to visit her husband. He refused to see her, so I gathered."

"And she didn't think of dropping in to wish me the time of day! Well, well! She's the limit!" Jules turned it with a laugh. "How about getting to bed now? We've all got jobs to do tomorrow. . . . Just you wait and see, Super. It ain't you who'll nab the murderer; it's this man here, Canut."

Charles nearly left his suitcase behind. It was Jules who reminded him of it. And he didn't get a chance of kissing Babette, because Superintendent Gentil accompanied him out.

"Have you seen my brother?" Charles asked, the minute they were in the street. A strong wind scattered sparks from the superintendent's cigarette.

"Yes; I saw him this morning."

"How is he?"

"He looks all right, but he absolutely refuses to speak to any of us; one might as well talk to a brick wall. He won't even see his lawyer. I understand he told the jailer that he'd bash Maître Abeille's face in if he came again."

They had reached the corner of Rue d'Etretat, where

their ways parted. And here the superintendent put the question that had been hovering on his lips all the time they were walking together.

"Tell me, Canut. Have you really discovered something?"

Charles, who had no idea how much Jules had told the police officer, temporized. "Maybe. But nothing definite so far."

"Well, if you do get on to anything, you'll pass me the word, won't you? I might be of help, you know."

"Thanks."

"Good night, Canut."

They shook hands. Carrying his suitcase, Charles turned off toward home, feeling in his pocket for the front-door key.

# 9

A NOTE in his cousin's writing was pinned to his bedroom door. "Your mother's at our place. You will find an apple turnover in the cupboard."

He ate the turnover because it was a tradition in the family that he had a passion for turnovers. Probably at some time in his childhood he had indulged in an orgy of them, and the memory had stuck. Anyhow, whenever there was one of them left over at closing time, his aunt would say, "We must keep it for Charles."

With these trivial thoughts he went to sleep, and on waking was again surprised to see it was broad daylight. For some reason he was reminded of the morning of Berthe's first communion. Why, he couldn't have said; presumably the air had had the same feel that morning.

He dressed rapidly. The bell gave its usual cheerful little peal as he entered the pastry shop. A moment later he was seated among the others at the round table in the back room. The sunbeams didn't reach here, but the door communicating with the shop had been left open and one could see the white tiles gleaming in the morning light.

An enormous blue enamel coffeepot stood in the center of the table. It had a brilliant silver band where the spout began, which had always fascinated Charles when he was little. As usual, caketrays lay on the chairs lining the wall and his uncle was reading the morning paper while he ate his breakfast.

"So, you see, he was quite frank about it," Charles concluded, after he had given an account of his experiences in Le Havre and his talk with Clovis Robin.

"I wouldn't be too sure about that," his aunt replied. "We know him better than you do. When it's a question of money, he'll say anything."

It was one of Madame Canut's "good days," as they called them. She looked sad but quite composed; her face had that air of gentle resignation that made her seem so fragile. Perhaps because of the brightness of the air or else because they were all seated around the table as if nothing were wrong, everyone was feeling less depressed this morning.

"What's your idea about the will?" asked Aunt Lou.

"I'm pretty sure," Charles replied, "that it was Paumelle who sent it."

"I didn't mean that. Do you think your mother should take the money or not?"

"Really, Louise!" protested Madame Canut.

"Oh, I know what you're going to say. But one shouldn't come to a hasty decision about things like that. Your sons might fall ill or lose their jobs; there's no knowing these days. Or one of them might have an accident. And then where would you be?"

"Oh, I'd go into the poorhouse."

Though the subject was a new one, the way they were discussing it was so much like dozens of conversations that had taken place *before* that Charles opened his eyes wide and looked around the room. It was like waking from a bad dream. Objects and people were all in their usual places, and the sun was shining. He would hardly have been surprised if the door had been flung open and Pierre had walked in, in his sea boots and oilskins, loudly announcing a number—that of the barrels of herring in the catch.

"Don't be absurd, dear. We'd never dream of letting you go to the poorhouse. All the same, something might happen to us, too, and then . . ."

Aunt Lou had a habit of talking about "something" that might happen, and it was never anything cheerful, always a catastrophe.

"If you want my opinion, the old man made that will because he felt remorseful. He wanted to atone. Anyhow, he did it quite as much for your sons' sake as for yours. Perhaps he hoped that God would forgive him. And in that case . . ."

"Louise!" sighed Madame Canut. "Please don't go on."

"Well," Charles pointed out, "the question won't really come up. Février was a married man, and his wife is claiming the estate."

"Let her claim it," said Monsieur Lachaume, looking up from his paper. "But she can't get around that there will. The court will see to that."

The words fell on deaf ears. The family had a settled conviction that, outside the bakery, Monsieur Lachaume was a negligible quantity. No one could deny that he was a worthy man and a skillful pastry cook, but he was hopelessly uneducated, and when he tried to air an opinion, they kindly but firmly shut him up.

"I can't imagine why they don't let Pierre out at once," said Madame Canut, looking at the sunlit street. Perhaps the sunshine, of which Pierre in his cell was now deprived, had prompted the remark. "Now that Paumelle's run away, I would have thought . . ."

She gave a start and rose to her feet. The others followed the direction of her gaze. They saw a man opening the street door and entering the shop with a rather embarrassed air. It was Monsieur Pessart. He coughed slightly, to attract the attention of the people in the back room.

144

Madame Lachaume hurried into the shop, whispering in her daughter's ear: "Take away the old coffeepot. Quick!"

Though convinced that it made better coffee than any other coffeepot, they were ashamed of its decrepitude.

"Do step inside, Monsieur Pessart. I'm afraid the room's dreadfully untidy, but we've only just finished breakfast."

"Is Charles here?"

"Yes. He's been having breakfast with us. Will you come this way?"

Lachaume, who was in his working clothes, had made himself scarce; Berthe had found time to take off her apron.

The shipowner bowed to Madame Canut.

"Good morning, madame. Good morning, mademoiselle . . . Sorry to disturb you at such an early hour, but I'd like to have a few words with Charles."

"Certainly. We'll go into the shop."

"No, no, that's quite unnecessary. There's nothing secret about it. The *Centaur* was due to sail this morning. But the crew are giving me trouble. They made difficulties last time, you know, and now they flatly refuse to go on board."

"I was told," Charles ventured to put in, "that they had a very poor haul last trip."

"That may be so, but it's no reason for laying up the boat. You know how they are. With your brother in command, everything ran like clockwork. That's why I've come here. I wonder if you could do something to make them see reason."

"Of course you will, Charles, won't you?" Aunt Lou had a pleased smile. "Won't you have a cup of coffee, Monsieur Pessart?"

"No, thanks. I've just had my breakfast."

"All right, sir," Charles said. "I'll come with you."

Monsieur Pessart's request had given him a little thrill

of pride, though he knew it was only because he was Pierre's brother that he had been approached. As they walked down the street side by side, he and the ship-owner, people turned to stare at them.

"There's been some talk of a demonstration outside the town hall to insist on your brother's being released. I made it clear that the mayor has no say in the matter. It's in the hands of the examining magistrate. . . . If only they could lay hands on that young scoundrel Paumelle!"

"Do you think he did it?" Charles asked eagerly.

"Well, that's the general idea. Isn't it yours?"

A few more steps took them to the harbor, which in the sunshine was a riot of cheerful colors—reds, greens, and blues. There was something almost sumptuous in the deep blue of the fishermen's clothes. They were standing in groups, their hands in their pockets, beside the bollards on the dock. The largest group was near the lock gate, just outside the Café de l'Amiral.

"Now then, Charles, it's up to you. Make them under-stand that by the time they're back from sea your brother will have been released. You might say that when you were in Rouen you gathered it was only a matter of . . . of certain formalities. After all, that's true enough, isn't it?"

Charles frowned slightly, but dared not protest. Monsieur Pessart was a shipowner, his brother's employer, and it was necessary to humor him.

Monsieur Pessart started by saying, "Here's Charles. Ask him to tell you about it. What was it you were saying just now, Charles?"

Charles felt at a loss; this unwonted cordiality from a "high-up" like Monsieur Pessart put him off stride. He tried to see if Babette was around, but only Jules stood in the doorway, watching the scene, his trousers, as usual, sagging down his paunch.

"My brother won't be in prison much longer," he announced firmly.

146

"That's good," said an old seaman who had known Charles almost from the cradle. "Got any news?"

Charles hesitated. He hardly liked to say yes, but he dared not say no in Monsieur Pessart's presence.

"Well, they know now he didn't do it. . . ."

"That's fine, but when will they let him out?"

The *Centaur* was there in the background, her hull mottled red where antirust paint had been applied. On her deck stood the skipper from Boulogne, who was looking far from proud of himself. He was waiting for the outcome of the discussion now in progress, hoping dubiously for the best.

"Pierre, let me tell you, would be mighty vexed if he knew the *Centaur* wasn't going to sea. And he'll be even angrier if, when he gets out, he finds her laid up for the season."

That Monsieur Pessart approved of this, he felt convinced, but he wasn't so sure about Jules, who appeared to be smiling sardonically. Or was it only the play of light and shadow on his face that gave him that look? Babette, too, had come out to watch. . . .

One of the crew put in a word. "Why didn't they arrest Paumelle right away? Looks as if they wanted to give him time to get away, don't it?"

"I can't say. I'm not in on the secrets of the police." He was one of them in the sense that he'd been to sea—but that was in his younger days, and they didn't wholly trust him.

"But suppose they let out Canut right away, and when he comes he finds we've sailed?"

"Even if he's released at once, he'll want some days off before going to sea again."

Monsieur Pessart signaled to him to go on talking, but he found nothing to add. Moving back a few steps, he left the crew to talk it out among themselves. The scene was a familiar one. Many of the men had packages of food under their arms. Here and there a woman with a child was chatting with her husband.

Two or three of the groups had separated from the others and were between him and Monsieur Pessart. Taking advantage of this opportunity, Charles made a move toward the Amiral. Jules grinned as he approached.

"So he went and hauled you out?"

"Yes. Just when I was having breakfast."

"And you didn't dare refuse, eh?"

"Well, what else could I do?"

"What, indeed?"

Charles disliked irony, perhaps because it was so alien to his own way of thought. When talking to the crew, he had been embarrassed by the smile on Jules's lips, and the man's present attitude was even more annoying.

"Don't you want to have a word with Babette?"

There was a note of amusement in the café owner's voice. Of course Charles wanted to have a word with Babette; what was so funny about that? When he reached her, she, too, started asking questions.

"Are they going to sail?"

"I don't know."

"Did he go to your place to get you?"

Charles wasn't conscious of being reproached for what he'd done, but he was certainly not being complimented. Probably he'd given the impression of being overly servile, and because there was a grain of truth in this, his depression increased.

"Didn't the super tell you anything yesterday evening?" Babette asked.

"No."

"He spent pretty nearly the whole day here. I almost wondered if he didn't suspect Jules of having had a hand in it."

She mentioned this quite casually, but Charles's heart missed a beat. Jules a suspect! It was a wholly new idea, and would never have crossed his mind without a suggestion from someone else. But, now he came to think of it, he had all along been rather mystified by the café owner's tactics.

Why had Jules dispatched him to Havre? And why had he professed such certainty that Charles, and only Charles, could trace the murderer? And, finally, why had he declared so positively that it couldn't have been Paumelle who did it?

Charles and Babette were in the café. Jules was still standing in the doorway, with his back to them, blocking out the sunlight.

Now he swung around and said to Charles: "Looks like they've decided to sail. . . . I imagine Monsieur Pessart wants to see you."

"If he does, he can come and see me here." And deliberately Charles sat down, just to show he wasn't at the ship-owner's beck and call.

"Give me some coffee, Babette."

Jules came in and planted himself in front of Charles. "Well?"

"Well what?"

"Found out anything more?"

"Not since last night." His tone was almost surly.

"Didn't the super have anything to tell you?"

"Should he?"

"Oh, I don't know. I only thought . . ."

Charles could have sworn the man had noticed his bad humor, guessed his suspicions—and was deliberately playing cat-and-mouse with him just to amuse himself.

"Ah, there he is. He wants you."

Monsieur Pessart had come to the door and was beckoning to Charles, because he never would set foot in a bistro. Despite his resolution, Charles rose a shade too promptly.

They walked together in the direction of the water-front.

"I'm obliged to you, Charles. They've agreed to sail on

149

condition that I double their bonus if the haul is under a thousand barrels."

But it was not only to thank him and to tell him this that Monsieur Pessart had called him. Charles guessed as much, and waited. "From what I hear, you're conducting a sort of inquiry on your own."

"Well, yes. I'm trying to find out the truth."

"I quite understand. But I can't help feeling that perhaps you're a bit handicapped—by your inexperience, for one thing. The amateur detective, you know . . ." He smiled.

While speaking, he kept an eye on the men on the *Centaur*'s deck.

"This is what I wanted to tell you," he went on. "You know my feelings toward your brother. He has always been in my employment, and it was I who made him what he is, a skipper. If you would like to call in someone, from Paris or elsewhere—a professional detective—I'll gladly foot the bill. And, of course, you'd co-operate with him."

For some reason this proposal had a disagreeable effect on Charles, who stared glumly at the ground, without replying.

"Well, think it over. And when you've made a decision, come to see me in my office." He held out his hand to Charles, and held the handshake a moment longer than usual, as though to seal a pact. "You may rest assured that I will spare no effort to get your brother set free."

It was one of those fine mornings that bring everybody out of doors. There was an easterly wind, and small fishing boats, which hadn't gone out for several weeks, were gliding across the harbor toward the open sea.

On board some big cod-fishing boats the crews were getting ready for the next voyage, carpenters, caulkers, and sailmakers moving about their decks. On the quay, two or three small rowboats, turned turtle, were being patched or painted by their owners. Some anglers were sitting at the end of the jetty, their legs dangling over the water.

Charles stood gazing across the harbor at the group of cottages in the second of which Tatine and her sister lived. Just beyond them was Emma's *estaminet*, and, to its left, behind a knoll, was the Villa des Mouettes; only its roof was visible, redder than the roofs of the neighboring house, from where Charles stood. He was conscious that something had changed in him during the last few hours —and that somehow his surroundings, too, had undergone a change. In the early phase, after his brother's arrest, he felt as if he had lived through a sort of cataclysm that had shattered his whole world to bits, beyond redress. But now the atmosphere of tragic suspense had given place to a sensation more like numbness. Vaguely he thought of a pond into which one has thrown a heavy stone and which, once the ripples have died away, becomes calm and stagnant as before.

When his eyes fell on the preparations going forward on the *Centaur*, he found, to his surprise, that he felt little or no distress at the thought that his brother wasn't in command this trip. Was it exhaustion, he wondered; or was it, instead, a perfectly natural human reaction that sometimes looks like callousness? He remembered how scandalized he had been, after attending funerals, at the way the mourners behaved on their return from the graveyard; how heartily they ate and drank—more heartily than usual, on the pretext that they needed cheering up.

Now that he came to think of it, he'd been behaving in much the same way. On the previous evening he'd polished off the whole apple turnover, a large one, and this morning he'd eaten a hearty breakfast while discussing the family tragedy almost as if it were an ordinary topic. And yet no one in the world could love Pierre as he did; that was unthinkable. They had come into the world together, and Charles had dedicated his whole life to his brother's service; indeed, at first he'd felt quite guilty when he asked Babette to marry him. . . .

After a while Monsieur Pessart's suggestion came back to his mind, and now he felt less hostile to it. Someone might well be called in from Paris—an expert used to tracking down criminals. He wouldn't make Charles's blunders or suffer, like Charles, from shyness; for instance, he'd know how to make old Tatine talk. As he walked along the waterfront, his eyes kept straying, almost wistfully, toward the old woman's cottage. There were all sorts of things, important things, Tatine must know. In fact, might she not know *all*?

He sighed. In his present mood, he felt singularly hopeless. All his zest, his resolution seemed to be melting away in the mild, warm sunshine. Just then a voice in his ears made him jump.

"Enjoying the air?"

It was the superintendent, looking rather drawn; he'd had a sleepless night.

"Well, yes. I was just having a walk."

"I wonder where that fellow Paumelle's gone to earth. I called Paris again this morning, but they hadn't traced him yet. Of course, all the railway stations are being watched and so are the ports."

Was Charles mistaken? He seemed to detect in his companion's voice something of his own lassitude.

"Well," sighed the superintendent, "we mustn't lose heart. The magistrate's going to question Février's cleaning woman again this morning, and perhaps he'll squeeze something out of her this time."

"Will he be coming here—to Fécamp?"

"No. She's been summoned to Rouen."

Charles was struck by the coincidence—that he and the magistrate had had the same idea at almost the same moment.

"I must go now. Let me remind you that I'm at your

disposal if at any time you want my help." And once again he started off in the direction of the Amiral—which gave color to Charles's theory that Jules was on the list of suspects.

Charles walked on. When he reached the end of the harbor, he saw Tatine, dressed up as though for a wedding or High Mass, hurrying toward the station. The sight of her set all sorts of ideas racing through his head; only to be ruled out, one by one, as hopelessly impractical.

It struck him, for instance, that quite likely Tatine's dressmaker sister was out for the day, working at somebody's house, as she did three or four times a week. In that case there would be no one in the cottage. Suppose he went in and had a look around? There was just the chance he might discover something useful. For almost five minutes he toyed with this project. It should be easy to get in through the back, breaking a window if necessary. Finally he dismissed the idea; he wasn't capable of adventure of that kind.

And what if, instead of breaking into the old women's cottage, he visited the Villa des Mouettes? Mightn't he hit on something there, a clue, as they called it in detective stories, that had escaped the police? Or why not call on Robin and have a straight talk with him, man to man? Robin certainly knew more than he admitted. . . . After all, hadn't Jules—who was no fool—said in the superintendent's presence that he, Charles, was the likeliest person to detect the murderer?

The noises of the harbor made a background to his musings. He had been walking with his eyes fixed on the ground. Now, looking up, he saw that he was near ˙the freight station, where he'd worked for years, and would probably go on working till the end of his days.

It struck him now that during the last forty-eight hours he'd hardly given a thought to Babette, whereas in the past he would spend three or four hours daily at a café table waiting for her to have a moment off and come talk to him. This, too, showed how greatly he had changed. He'd been the sort of man who settles into a groove and seems incapable of swerving from it. Well, he'd been jolted out of it, all right; never would he be able to resume life on the old lines or see things as before.

The difference was that hitherto he'd taken everything at its face value, so to speak, and never looked beneath the surface. Jules was a case in point. He'd tacitly assumed that Jules had been and always would be as he was today. Now he knew better; he knew that Jules had once been a waiter and had had an affair with Georgette. Then Georgette had gone to South America, where she met Février. And then . . .

Also there was that unpleasant young man Paumelle. Somehow he must be fit into the picture. The extraordinary thing was his sending back that will—the last thing one would expect him to do, if he were the murderer. Wait, though! Mightn't it be that he wanted to make things blacker for the Canuts by showing that they had an interest in Février's death?

He had walked past Tatine's cottage without pausing. A little farther on a woman was cleaning her windows, standing on a ladder and providing a lavish display of leg. Charles caught himself staring, and blushed. Has a man any right to think of such things when his brother is in jail?

The curtains of Emma's window were drawn. On a sudden impulse he entered her little café. The room was empty. A skein of mustard-yellow wool lay on the table.

He felt immediately that something was different, but at first didn't know what it was. A moment later, on approaching the stove, he noticed it was unlit. That was the difference; the room was cold, and its coldness made it seem emptier. He went up to the door at the far end.

"Is anyone in?"

"Who's there?" The Flemish woman's voice came from the top of the stairs.

"A customer."

"I'm coming down."

But she didn't come down, and Charles could hear her shuffling about in the room overhead. It sounded as if she was making her bed.

When finally she came down, she seemed taken aback at seeing Charles. She was dressed to go out, in black silk and enormous earrings.

"What do you want?"

"I'd like a drink, please." Charles sat down at one of the tables.

"Do you propose to stay a couple of hours, like you did last time?"

"Maybe. I don't know."

The thick crochetwork curtains cut the sunlight into squares, small near the window, then progressively bigger. They made a symmetrical pattern covering floor and tables, Emma's dress and face.

"What do you want to drink?"

"Some cider, please."

"You know quite well I don't keep cider."

"Then beer."

She made no secret of her anger, and slammed a glass down in front of him so hard that it almost broke. Then she stood beside his chair and glowered down on him.

"Why do you keep poking your nose in where you aren't wanted?"

Taken off guard, Charles fumbled for a reply, then raised the glass to his lips.

"I was feeling thirsty and I . . ."

"Nonsense! We all know where *you* go when you want a drink. Spend all your evenings there, don't you? Hanging around a bit of skirt? That'll be a franc." She held out her hand, to signify that she expected him to pay, finish his drink, and go. "Maybe you're going to ask where Paumelle is? Well, he ain't here, I can tell you that. And where he is is nobody's business."

Charles found nothing to say. But he guessed that the woman's nerves were stretched and he'd do well to stay, unpleasant though this was, on the off chance . . .

"Well? Do you propose to sit there like a stuck pig all morning?"

"Really, I don't understand why . . ."

"Because, if you do, I'm off. I got better things to do than keep you company—for a franc's worth of beer."

Looking at her eyes, he felt sure she had been crying. Naturally enough, no doubt, if Paumelle had been her lover. Just then he had a flash of inspiration. Her annoyance when he came, her eagerness for him to leave, and the fact that she was in her best clothes—all these had an obvious explanation: she was going to meet Paumelle, wherever he was. For she, if anyone, knew his whereabouts.

He finished his drink hastily.

"All right. I'm going now."

"High time!"

He felt certain she, too, would be leaving almost immediately. He'd shadow her, learn where Paumelle was hiding, and promptly inform the police. And once Paumelle was arrested, they'd be bound to set Pierre free.

He took up a stand in a small side street, in a patch of shadow; from this point he had a clear view of the road leading to town. Two dogs were scampering around, rolling on their backs, snapping at each other in play. He found he could think more clearly now that he was in the open. Emma was, almost certainly, intending to take a train, and if she did, he would board it, too.

What a relief to have a definite plan! But his relief was short-lived; looking toward a nearby cottage window, he saw a big moon face behind the curtains, and his spirits

156

dropped. It was Tatine's sister, eying him like a fat spider watching its next victim from the center of its web.

However, he mastered his first impulse to move. Let her watch him, if it amused her! In the clear, bright air all sorts of homely sounds came to his ears. Someone was beating a carpet at an upper window; in a yard a woman was chopping firewood; quite nearby a baby was whimpering and an onion stew was sizzling on a stove. It struck him that this was probably the first day for weeks that people had their windows open.

But all the time, he was listening for other sounds—a closing door and someone coming down the road. Emma would have to pass quite near him, and after giving her, say, thirty yards' start, he could start shadowing her.

Half an hour, an hour went by, and still the old woman kept watch at her window, sometimes pressing her nose against it—which made the big, flat face still more grotesque. But there was no sign of Emma.

Could he have been mistaken about her intention of going out? Perhaps she'd put her black dress on for some other purpose. Of course, she might have taken the road in the opposite direction, turned to the right on leaving her house. But that road led only to the beach. Still, it was just possible to walk along the beach and get to town that way. But she wasn't likely to do that, especially in her best clothes.

The dogs were tired of playing with each other, and one of them was gazing up at Charles appealingly, with the obvious hope that he would throw a stick. It was a small reddish-brown mongrel with a curly tail wagging expectantly.

Clocks were striking eleven. A door closed, and there was the sound of footsteps; but it was only a housewife, shopping net in hand, who walked briskly past. She gave a glance up the side street as she went by, as though she'd sensed Charles's presence in the patch of shadow.

Next came a group of children hurrying home from

school; three boys and a girl. They stopped and gaped at Charles for a moment, ran on, and looked back again before turning in at a gate. Evidently they told their mother about the man hiding up the side street, because a young woman came out and eyed him suspiciously for some minutes, then started talking to someone in the next house.

Charles blushed for shame at the idea that these good women suspected him of—heaven knew what! Afraid he might be asked what he was up to, he emerged from his retreat and walked slowly back toward Emma's.

When he turned the handle, he found the door locked. Peeping in through the window, he saw nothing except the empty glass where he had left it. When rattling the door and rapping on the window had no effect, he moved back to have a look at the upper floor. All the windows were shut.

The women who had been watching him were still standing at their gates, some twenty yards away. One of them called to him: "She's not in."

"Are you sure?"

"Yes, of course I am. I saw her leave a quarter of an hour ago."

"What?"

"She went down to the pier and crossed in the ferry."

That was the one thing he hadn't reckoned on. He'd completely forgotten the existence of the ferry, which saved one a long walk around the harbor. The two women couldn't understand his consternation.

"Oh, she'll be back in the afternoon, I expect," one of them said.

He wanted to say something to them, but could think of nothing. So he thanked them with a slight nod and a smile, and hurried back to town in a curious mood, between elation and despondency. It certainly looked as though his intuitions were correct. On reaching the Amiral, he promptly looked around for the superintendent; but the police officer wasn't at his usual place.

"What's up?" Jules asked.

"Oh . . . nothing."

"Did you want to see the super?"

"Well, I'd thought . . ."

"You're too late, my boy. He's just left. Paumelle's been found, and he dashed off to see him."

Jules seemed to be chuckling over his discomfiture; Babette was busy serving four customers who were playing cards on the far side of the room.

# 10

"I'M SURE you're going to do something silly—again! Well, that's your business."

Babette had wound up their conversation on this discouraging note. Nevertheless, she had given him the money he'd asked for, because he didn't want to waste time going home. And she came to the door with him. Jules shouted after him, "Where are you off to?" but Charles merely waved his hand.

"May I borrow your bicycle for a while, Monsieur Martin?"

Hardly waiting for the answer, he jumped on it, and, pedaling with his back down like a racing cyclist, threading his way between cars and trucks, reached the passenger station in record time.

"Has the Dieppe train left?" he panted.

The porter pointed; it was still in. Leaving the bicycle against a wall, he bought a ticket, then hurried along the platform, peeping into each compartment. It was an old-fashioned local train, without a corridor.

When he saw what he was looking for, he opened the door of the compartment and jumped in, despite the protests of three market women who had dumped their baskets of vegetables on the seats.

His heart was thudding, no less with emotion than with the strain of his rush to the train. When, leaning back, he shut his eyes for a moment, he could still see, as distinctly as if they were wide open, the fat Flemish woman sitting in the seat in front of his.

THIS HAD taken place at twelve-thirty. Charles had remembered just in time that there was only one train at this hour of the day, the slow one to Dieppe. And, despite Babette, despite Jules's superior smiles, his guess had proved correct: Emma was certainly involved in the crime.

"I'm sure you're going to do something silly—again!" Really, Babette had no business saying that, if only in her own interest. There are moments when casual remarks strike deeper and wound more than at normal times, and just now Charles was exceptionally vulnerable. Why that "again"? Had he done so many silly things before? Or was it Jules who had created a legend of his "silliness"?

And why, since she knew next to nothing, far less than he did, about this business, couldn't she have shown some confidence in him, instead of carping?

No, he told himself, he wasn't offended or estranged, but somehow his mental picture of Babette was—how should he put it?—losing glamour. He almost saw her now as a foolish little chit who, merely because he'd talked about marrying her, fancied she had the right to sit in judgment on him.

Angrily he switched his mind to less dismal thoughts. And anyway, there was something about this train that prevented one from keeping one's mind long on the same subject. It was constantly stopping. Already there had been four stops: Fécamp–Saint-Ouen, Colleville, Valmont, Ourville. . . . As he watched Emma wearily, from the corner of an eye, it struck him that she had changed since morning and was looking definitely older.

With her earrings as big as pigeons' eggs, her glossy silk dress, her three bangles, and a huge gold locket rising and falling on her ample bosom, she looked grotesque, and the market women had no compunction about exchanging amused glances. Another detail they had certainly noticed was that Emma's hair was a totally different color at the roots—which, of course, showed that she dyed it.

When Charles looked down, his eyes fell on a pair of new patent-leather shoes with unusually high heels, above which bulges of fat protruded.

"Ain't there no first-class in this train?" asked one of the market women, with a scornful glance at Emma's finery.

The situation became more embarrassing for Charles when the women left the train at Heberville. He very nearly beckoned to a man who hovered outside the door for a moment, as if about to enter, but unfortunately thought better of it.

So when the train drew out, Charles found himself confronting Emma in a closed space with no way of escape. Let's only hope, he thought, she hasn't got a revolver. She'd be quite capable of killing me out of hand. Looking up, he saw a large suitcase on the rack, obviously Emma's. When presently he shifted his gaze to her face, he could have sworn she'd been growing uglier every moment since she boarded the train. What gave this impression was that the makeup seemed to be peeling off her cheeks. She had put it on in blobs, and the mascara on her eyelashes had granulated, giving the effect of small black beads stuck on haphazardly. And somehow, at this moment, his suspicion that she was Février's murderer became a certainty.

Why? For one thing, he couldn't see Paumelle cutting the old man's throat. He might have knocked him on the head or stabbed him, but as for slitting his throat . . . no, that wouldn't be Paumelle's way. Nor, indeed, if he had been the killer, would he have sent back the will or brought more suspicion on himself by leaving town abruptly.

That, of course, proved nothing against Emma. But logic played little part in Charles's certainty. The one definite thing he had to go on was that Emma was in a panic; hence her flight. And his presence in the seat facing her evidently added to her alarm; though the compartment was quite cold, she was now sweating profusely.

He had no plan; everything would depend on her next move. Probably she meant to take the boat to England or the train to Belgium. Or perhaps she didn't know herself where she was going; on the whole, that seemed the likeliest theory. In any case, she had the look of someone on the brink of doing something desperate, taking an irremediable step. Charles now had another fear—that she would suddenly open the door and jump out.

At Offranville a priest by himself was pacing the platform. When Emma saw him, she touched wood. Though some compartments were empty, the priest picked the one where Charles and Emma were, and settled down in the corner seat farthest from hers. There was one other small station; then Dieppe. Emma reached up awkwardly to her suitcase. Charles didn't dare volunteer, but the priest came to her aid.

"Allow me . . ."

The suitcase appeared to be heavy. Nonetheless, on leaving the station, Emma didn't take a taxi. As she walked up the slight incline leading toward the quays, her high heels kept turning over, and Charles could almost feel his ankles aching in sympathy.

Though she must have known he was following, she never turned her head. Both of them heard three short blasts of a steamer's whistle. The woman tried to quicken her pace, but merely stumbled, and when she reached the quay, the Newhaven steamer was edging her way across the harbor toward the narrow fairway between the jetties.

She stopped and looked around like someone who has

no more reason to go in one direction than in another. It was half past two. There was much more animation here than in the surroundings of Fécamp's harbor, and the air was loud with the stridence of a record player in one of the cafés near the docks.

A few moments later Emma had settled down in a corner of this café. She looked so tired and miserable that Charles had a twinge of compunction. Nevertheless, he took a seat not far from hers, and presently saw her gulping down a glass of neat brandy.

At half past three she ordered a sandwich, but couldn't get through more than half of it. For some reason Babette's remark "You're going to do something silly—again!" came back to him. She'd had no business saying a thing like that. And now he caught himself viewing her critically, like an outsider.

Her looks were nothing much; Jules was right there. She had skimpy hips and small breasts. Even the faint warm odor that came from her in bed had nothing to commend it. Then why did the mere recollection of that odor make his senses tingle? . . .

The situation became absurd. Emma rose and walked to the toilet, and so scared was Charles by the thought of her eluding him that he actually followed. He posted himself beside the door and, when she came out, pretended to be washing his hands.

Unlike the Fécamp cafés, this one was nothing if not up-to-date. Beside the woman at the cashier's desk was the record player, which was hooked up to two loudspeakers, one above the bar and another facing the street. The cashier changed the records.

Emma asked for a railway timetable, studied it carefully, then pushed it away with a despondent gesture. After this she called the manager and had a whispered conversation with him. Anyhow, Charles reflected, if she was asking about the next boat for Newhaven, there wouldn't be one for many hours yet, not till nine-fifteen.

THE LIGHTS had been on for quite a while, and Charles was beginning to feel rather torpid, what with the heat, the strident music, and his forced inactivity. Little by little the café had filled up with people dropping in for short drinks before dinner. Half unconsciously, he had been following the progress of a card game at the next table. The players were a queer, shriveled old fellow with a big wart on his nose and a robust-looking man of whom Charles had only a back view.

Had anyone abruptly asked him what he was doing here, he'd have been hard put to it to answer. All he knew was that he was still waiting, as for hours and hours he had been waiting. And at her table, Emma, after having finished a novel with a gaudy cover that she'd extracted from her bag, was waiting, too.

The door opened, as it had every minute or so, sending a gust of cold air against Charles's legs; he had chosen a bad place. This time it was a boy who entered, with the evening papers. Charles bought one; so did Emma. They unfurled their papers at exactly the same moment, and the eyes of both fell on a headline:

SENSATIONAL DEVELOPMENT
IN THE FÉCAMP MURDER CASE
PAUMELLE ACCUSES HIS MISTRESS
OF THE CRIME

IT SEEMED that everyone had been mistaken about him. Paumelle had had the reputation of being a young tough, capable of anything. Actually, when arrested in Poitiers, he had not protested. He had no idea where he was, having been in such a hurry that he'd got on the wrong train.

"Well, you've got me," he sighed, and caused no trouble when they fastened handcuffs on his wrists. "Believe me or not, I swear I wasn't trying to make a getaway. So she's in for it, the old girl. Anyhow, she can't say I didn't warn her."

These details and others were quoted in the newspaper, whose special correspondent had phoned them in. Paumelle had been taken to a detective inspector, who had put him through the usual grilling.

"Why did you kill Février?"

"You're wasting your breath. I didn't kill the old man."

"In that case, how did you come to be in possession of his will?"

"His will?"

"We have evidence to show that you sent it by mail, after cutting out the magistrate's address from a newspaper."

"Well, what if I did?"

"What did you do with the money and securities?"

For a quarter of an hour, no more than that, he held out. Finally he said: "Look! Give me some grub and drinks first, lots of drinks, and then perhaps I'll spill the beans."

He grinned at his audacity. After a hasty meal, in the course of which he asked for and was given a second bottle of wine, he demanded cigarettes.

"That's better. Now I suppose I'd better begin at the beginning."

The drinks and the warmth of the room, after his many hours in the open, had flushed his cheeks.

"I don't need to tell you about the wreck of the *Télémaque* and what happened after that; it's all been in the papers, hasn't it? . . . I bet if that sort of thing had happened to you—if you'd made a meal off an Englishman, I mean—you'd feel queer afterward."

And in a tone in which there was more than mere facetiousness—some subtle, undefined emotion—he added: "So I can say I've got English blood in my veins."

Then he ran his eyes over their faces, and took another drink of wine.

"Anyhow, my father never really got over it, and one night he came to a pretty horrible end, squashed to a jelly between his boat and the harbor wall. . . . So I was left on my own, and maybe I might have made something of my life, as they say. . . . For a while I thought of enlisting; but I knew I couldn't face army discipline. . . . There's no need to go into details, but I want you to notice that I never got into trouble with the cops—which means I didn't do anything so very bad. . . . Ten years ago old Février came to live in Fécamp. I'd probably never have got to know him, in spite of that business of the *Télémaque* and my father's having been his shipmate, if he hadn't got into the habit of going to see Emma."

His voice was thickening as a result of the wine, and he spoke in a bored tone, as if he thought it hardly worth the trouble, going into these details of the past.

"You'll see for yourselves what Emma's like. . . . She's long in the tooth, I grant you, but she's a good sort in her way, and, between ourselves, quite a nice piece to go to bed with. Anyhow, there are half a dozen men in Fécamp —married men, mostly, with proper jobs and the rest of it—who make no bones about going to her place two or three times a week. . . . Of course I was different; I had my own reasons."

"You mean, you were her lover?"

He gave a drunken guffaw. "Lover! It always makes me laugh when I hear people say that. It ain't the right word . . . Still, you can call me that if you want; it's near enough. She made a fuss over me, cooked me nice little dinners, and when I hadn't a centime, she'd fork out something. . . . We can't all be skippers of fishing boats, you know—or railway clerks."

"What do you mean by that?"

"Never mind. It'd take too long to explain."

For a moment his eyes hardened, and he seemed lost in thought.

"It was she who told me about the old boy and the sort

167

of life he led. A dog's life, it seemed to me. Sometimes for weeks on end he'd shut himself up and not say a word to anyone—except Emma. . . . He'd fallen for her, you know: You'd have thought he was past that sort of thing, but there's some old men keep it up to their dying day."

The inspector tried to stop him from filling up his glass again, but, bottle in hand, he eyed him defiantly. "What does it matter to you if I get drunk, so long as I tell you what I know about the murder? That's what you're after, isn't it? . . . Where was I? Yes . . . Well, one day, when he was down in the mouth, like he often was, Février came out with the whole yarn. He told Emma it was that *Télémaque* business that he'd never got over, it preyed on his mind, and so on and so forth.

"That gave me a bright idea. I went to his place one afternoon and told him a lot of sob stuff—how my father had died of a broken heart, and nobody in town would have anything to do with me, so I couldn't get a job, and I'd half a mind to drown myself in the harbor.

"It did the trick, all right. The old boy coughed up five hundred francs the first time. After that he gave me smaller sums, off and on, a hundred one day, fifty another. . . . A queer card he was. He always looked so green about the gills, like he had fish's blood in his veins. Dead and alive. But in spite of that, he was terribly afraid of dying and was always reading medical books.

"Now, wait a minute! I must try to remember exactly what led up to it. . . . I suppose people will say I've got my knife into Emma, but it ain't so. She was always very decent to me; but that's no reason why I should make her a present of my neck.

"It'll make you laugh when I tell you she had got it into her head she could persuade Février to marry her. She was after his money, of course, but the house was what she really wanted. She'd always wanted to have a proper house of her own, and she had a special fancy for Février's." He laughed. "You'd call it her 'fancy house.'

"Only—the old boy wasn't having any. . . . He flatly refused to marry her. The trouble was that Emma had set her heart on it. She froze out her other men and made a dead set at Février. Maybe she felt she was getting a little old for that sort of thing and it was time to settle down. . . .

"'Anyhow,' she once told me, 'I'll make him leave it to me in his will.' And she kept on asking me to pump him about his intentions.

"I couldn't help her there; I didn't try to, for that matter. But I did tell her one day about Février's planning to leave the place. That loony, Madame Canut, was getting on his nerves; he'd had enough of being preached at in the street. His idea was to sell his house and clear out. . . . I don't know where to; maybe South America. . . .

"Next time he came to see her, Emma made a hell of a scene. I may as well tell you she has another mania, has Emma; she's always threatening people that she'll 'have the law on them.' And, what's more, she does it. She ran in the woman next door because her dog had messed on her doorstep. That's how she is. . . .

"Well, she told Février he had no business leaving her in the lurch like that, after he'd taken advantage of her and ruined her good name and so forth. . . . It sounds damn silly, but she really seemed to think she had a 'good name.' Anyhow, she was always harping on it. . . .

"Then it happened—I mean they found the old boy with his throat slit, and Canut was arrested. I swear to you I didn't know a thing about it. Likely as not, I spent that evening at the Amiral, watching Canut—the other one—he's a railway clerk and a real sap—getting redder and redder in the face because I was making up to his girl, that kid Babette. . . .

"I won't deny that next day, when I heard that Captain Canut had been arrested, I smelled a rat. But it was no business of mine. . . . And Emma, too, didn't give herself away. She went on sitting for hours at the window, knitting, like she always did. But I guessed when, two days after it happened, she asked me if it was true one could get forged passports made.

" 'Why do you want to know that?' I asked her.

" 'Oh, for nothing in particular. I read about it in a story.'

"She always read novels when she was knitting; she said it helped her.

"Then she said to me, 'It seems there's some people who have a marvelous knack of copying any kind of writing. I'd like to meet one.'

"I asked her: 'Why?'

"Mind you, she knew quite well she'd need my help sooner or later. But she wasn't going to come out with it all at once. . . . She was a deep one, was old Emma.

"For two days she kept mum, then one afternoon she asked me to come up to her bedroom, and I thought it was for the usual thing because she bolted the front door.

" 'There's only some words want changing,' she said to me, and held out a sheet of paper.

"I had a real shock when I saw what it was. The old boy's will!

" 'He brought it on himself. He was going to play a nasty trick—clear out without leaving me a centime.'

"Well, I must say I couldn't help admiring her. A cool customer, that she was! For four days she'd kept mum, and never turned a hair—with all that on her mind! . . .

"Then she says to me: 'There's some sort of acid that takes away ink, ain't there? Suppose you go to Paris and hunt up someone who knows the trick? I can't go, of course. They'd start suspecting things, if I went off like that. But as long as Canut's in the clink, they'll leave us in peace.'

"I didn't like that 'us.' There's some things I draw the line at, though you may not think so. I asked her what she'd done with the cash and securities.

" 'Don't you worry your head about that; I've got them in a safe place.'

170

"That was Emma all over. She couldn't trust anybody, not even me. All she wanted was for me to do that job in Paris.

"Well, at first I said, 'Nothing doing.' . . . Then I noticed that Canut, the one who's with the railway, kept following me around, and I began to feel I'd like a change of air. So I said to Emma: 'A job like that must cost a lot of money.'

" 'I'll pay what's needed.'

" 'How much?'

" 'Five thousand down. And five thousand after.'

" 'Okay,' I said. 'Hand it over.'

"So that was that. I pocketed the five thousand and cleared out. My idea was to get to Marseilles and take a boat. I had a vague notion of joining the Foreign Legion. With my three or four thousand francs I'd be on easy street—to start with, anyway.

"Emma had given me the will and I didn't know what to do with it. I'd half a mind to burn it, and that's what I would have done if Madame Canut hadn't been a loony. You see, I'm not trying to whitewash myself; I'm talking straight. But they say it brings bad luck if you do dirt to a loony. Sounds silly, maybe, but I wasn't going to risk it.

"So I mailed the will to Rouen. . . . I was a bit flurried that night and took the wrong train. At one of the stops I found it out, and just when I was changing your man nabbed me. . . . So now you know!"

He smiled, and the smile implied: Well, now you know the sort of man I am. I may not be a plaster saint, but I've never done anything so very terrible.

CHARLES SEEMED to come out of a dream. He looked around him in a puzzled way, wondering where he was. Then his gaze settled on Emma, who, carrying her suitcase, was threading her way between the tables.

She was heading again for the toilet. He heard the outer door open and close; then an inner one. For some moments he stayed quite still. Then suddenly he sprang to his feet and hurried across the café to the toilet. The door was closed, and the word *Engaged* showed above the latch.

"Are you there?" he asked, hardly knowing what he said.

Silence. Listening carefully, he seemed to hear moans inside.

He lunged against the door with his shoulder, with no result. So he hurried back to the café and whispered some words in the manager's ear. People were staring; Charles's face betrayed his agitation. The manager, too, seemed agitated; he rushed to the lavatory, returned, and ran his eyes around the room, looking for someone.

"Robert! Come quick!"

The man addressed was the robust cardplayer. He got up, still holding his cards.

There was another whispered conversation. The three of them, now in the narrow little room, could distinctly hear groans, all the more ominous for their feebleness, behind the door marked *Engaged*.

Robert stepped back, then launched himself against the door with all his might. The lock gave way at his third attempt. Huddled on the floor lay a woman, with splintered glass on her black dress, blood on her hands.

Emma hadn't lost consciousness. Her face was not contorted, and her groans seemed almost mechanical, as if there was no pain behind them. She looked up at the three men like someone in a dream.

"Call a doctor. Quick!"

The manager and his friend found Charles's presence irksome. He seemed to be always in their way and kept asking futile questions. "What has she done to herself?" "Do you think she's dying?"

More people crowded in. All the customers in the café were on their feet, and for some time no one thought of switching off the record player. At last a doctor appeared, and he had Emma carried upstairs to a bedroom.

Charles was not allowed to go up; no one knew that he was anything more than an ordinary customer. He remained in the lavatory and, though he tried to look elsewhere, his eyes kept straying to the bloodstains on the floor, and he felt like vomiting. When he saw someone picking up a patent-leather shoe, he suddenly exclaimed: "Send for the police. I have something to tell them. It's terribly important."

To his dismay, Charles found himself greeted by hostile looks. His intervention had evidently roused the darkest suspicions against him. He was relieved to see a policeman's cap appear behind the group hemming him in. The policeman promptly fished a bulky notebook from his pocket.

"It's Emma," Charles panted, before the man had had time to speak. "The woman all the papers are talking about. The one who killed Février." And, hardly knowing what he said, he added hastily: "They're looking after her all right, aren't they? It would be so dreadful if she died."

The truth was that he was almost beginning to regard himself as a murderer. Hadn't he hounded the wretched woman to her death? He was trembling so violently that he had to sit down.

"Drink that. No, do as you're told. At one gulp."

It was something strong and pungent. The man they called Robert came down the stairs. Charles tried to hear what he said, but could catch only some disconnected phrases.

". . . hidden her glass in her bag . . . cut a vein in her wrist . . ."

"Will she die?"

Charles noticed a hint of suspicion in the policeman's eye as well.

"How is it you know so much about it?"

"Oh . . . I'm Canut, his brother. That's why I came here."

To his mind this explained everything. But no; nobody seemed to understand or even try to understand.

"Look!" he exclaimed. "Can you *do* something? . . . Telephone to—someone."

Suddenly a picture rose before him of the Flemish woman leaving the station, toiling up the hill with her heavy suitcase, stumbling over the cobblestones, turning her high heels. And it was the last straw.

"I'm going to be sick!" he warned the people near him, who moved hastily away.

And there, in the middle of the café, he brought up what little he had eaten over the sawdust-strewn floor.

# 11

THE MADDENING thing was that the last train had left. He
had nothing more to do here, but how was he to get back
to Fécamp?

At the police station, where he had told them all he
knew, he looked so woebegone that they insisted on his
drinking a cup of strong black coffee.

While he was there, he heard the latest news of Emma;
she was in the hospital and, according to the doctor, out
of danger.

"You can go now," Charles had been told. "No doubt
the examining magistrate will want a statement from you,
but we have no more questions."

He reached the quay just as the Newhaven boat was
leaving, with all her lights on. The first thing, he decided,
was to call Fécamp, and, since the Lachaumes had no
telephone, he'd have to call the Amiral.

The idea of returning to the café of gruesome associ-
ations, where the loudspeaker was blaring away again,
offended him, so he went into another establishment.
Closing the narrow door of the telephone booth behind
him, he had a disagreeable feeling; it was reminiscent of a
door that he had vainly tried to open.

"Hello! Is this the Amiral?"

The telephone exchange began by saying there was no answer, and Charles grew exasperated.

"That's nonsense! It's a café, and it can't possibly be closed so early."

"All right, I'll try again."

This time, a voice he didn't recognize said gruffly: "Yes? What do you want?"

"Is this the Café de l'Amiral? . . . Good. Will you ask Babette to come to the phone?"

"What's that?"

"But—damn it! Look! Am I speaking to the Café de l'Amiral?"

"Yes, but there's no one here."

Charles guessed that the person at the other end of the line wasn't used to telephoning.

"Listen! I want to speak to the girl who works at the Amiral."

"This is the Amiral."

"Who's speaking, please?"

"Eh? I didn't catch . . ."

"I want to know who's speaking."

"Oscar."

"Oscar who? Isn't Jules there?"

"No, he's out."

"And Babette?"

"She's out, too."

"What? Both of them?"

"See here! What do you want?"

What did he want? He wanted to talk to someone, obviously. And he couldn't make out why the café should be empty at nine in the evening.

"Where have they gone?"

"Who?"

"Jules and Babette."

"They're at the dock."

"Can't you shout to them to come?"

"No. They're too far away—in front of Monsieur Pessart's house. They've gone to see Canut; he's just come back."

Charles felt like weeping with frustration. Receiver in hand, he stared dully in front of him, incapable of getting another word out. Here he was, marooned in Dieppe, while Pierre was at Fécamp, and everybody in town had gone to see him!

He couldn't know, of course, that Monsieur Pessart had driven to Rouen in his car to fetch Pierre, or that some three hundred people had gathered outside the shipowner's house, or that his mother had been sent for, and had come, escorted by Aunt Lou and Berthe.

When leaving the café, he nearly forgot to pay. Then, as often happens in such moments of bewilderment, a fantastic notion crossed his mind. What a pity he hadn't brought that bicycle with him instead of leaving it in Fécamp! Fantastic, because it would have taken him the whole night to do the journey on a bicycle.

Somehow the thought of hiring a car didn't occur to him. Of course, he'd never taken a taxi in his life. But when he was walking along the quay, past the red façade of the market, he noticed three cars, each with a small white flag up. The drivers went on talking to each other, never suspecting that the young man was a potential fare.

"How much would you charge to take me to Fécamp?"

They exchanged glances, then worked it out between them.

"Four hundred francs."

And so, a moment later, he was sitting in an antiquated private car, which still flaunted cut-glass flower vases with artificial carnations in them, relics of its heyday.

At Monsieur Pessart's house, lights shone from all the windows of the upstairs rooms. Those who had any sort of claim to do so had gone inside, but the majority had stayed in the street. Among the latter was Babette, who kept very close to Jules, as if she were afraid of being lost in the crowd.

Inside, they were drinking champagne. The mayor had come, and his car, with the chauffeur at the wheel, was drawn up at the gate.

Everyone was drinking toasts. "Here's luck to you, Canut!" "Bravo, Canut!"

And Monsieur Pessart, who made a point of staying at Pierre's side, was shepherding him toward the window.

"Go and show yourself on the balcony and say a few words to them."

Looking, as he felt, terribly embarrassed by all this to-do, of which he was the focus, Pierre shuffled forward. There was a cheerful roar from the crowd when they saw him at the window.

It was one of those chaotic occasions when nobody quite knows what he is doing and decorum goes by the board. Monsieur Pessart had let people whom ordinarily he'd never have allowed to cross his threshold invade his house. What was more, they were being served champagne. On a sofa, Madame Canut sat weeping quietly, with Madame Pessart beside her, murmuring consolation and sometimes patting her shoulder. The mayor was exchanging amenities with Berthe Lachaume, who normally did no more than pack up cakes for him.

"Where's Charles?" Pierre had asked eagerly on his arrival, but no one could enlighten him.

"For the last week we haven't seen much of him. He's been on the move all the time, trying to find out something, of course. Nobody knows where he's gone today."

No one spoke of going home to bed. There was something incoherent about it all, and Pierre looked half dazed.

"Your brother's been splendid," said Monsieur Pessart, who this evening made a point of giving Pierre his arm frequently, as if he were a woman—which was all the more amazing because expansiveness of this kind was not at all like Monsieur Pessart.

"Yes? What's he been doing?"

"Well, for one thing, he helped me persuade the crew to sail. They'd refused to budge as long as you were away."

Most exceptional of all, perhaps, was Monsieur Pessart's appearance; his eyes were sparkling, his cheeks were flushed, and he looked ten years younger. Normally a most abstemious drinker, he had had several glasses of old brandy with Monsieur Laroche when he went to Rouen to get Pierre.

The magistrate had been all affability.

"I trust there's no ill will. If I deprived you of your best skipper for a few days, it really couldn't be helped. . . . Canut behaved very well; he gave us no trouble. . . . The only thing I have against him is that he was—how shall I put it?—a trifle unjust toward Maître Abeille, who really did his best."

Everyone wanted to drink with Pierre, who didn't dare refuse, so he accepted the glasses that were handed him with a rather sheepish smile.

"Here's luck, old boy. Anyhow, you look none the worse for your spell of 'doing time.' "

No. He looked exactly as in the past. And, since he'd shaved that morning, his cheeks were as smooth as when he put on his best clothes and went for a stroll in town after returning from a fishing expedition.

"I think your friends down there would like to have a word with you," Monsieur Pessart suggested, pointing to the street. The clock had just struck eleven.

Pierre wondered what he should do: go home with his mother or join his friends outside and make a night of it at the Amiral. He had a vague feeling that the night's felicity was lacking something, but he had drunk too much to realize that what he missed was Charles.

A minute or two later he was on the quay, hardly knowing how he'd got there, and kissing Babette, who was smiling shyly up at him. If the kiss was needlessly prolonged, that, too, was because of the champagne.

"You'll come along with us for a drink?" someone suggested.

Of course he would! And while they set out toward the Amiral, Charles, seated in his taxi, was absently watching the long glare of the headlights on the dark country road, and still picturing, much against his will, the squat black form of the Flemish woman huddled on the floor of the badly lighted little lavatory. And that shoe of hers that someone had picked up . . . !

He was half asleep by the time they entered Fécamp, and, when they reached the quay, failed to notice that Monsieur Pessart's house was now in darkness.

The driver stopped and said, over his shoulder: "Will this do? Or where do you want me to take you?"

Only the mayor's car was to be seen. Evidently the two bigwigs were rounding off the evening with a talk in one of the back rooms.

Charles roused himself with an effort. "Thanks. I'll get out here."

It went against the grain to hand over four hundred francs for a journey that would have cost him only thirty-eight by train. He was feeling depressed, too, and was vexed with himself for feeling so.

Even at this distance he could see that a festive gathering was in progress at the Amiral.

A new thought waylaid him. Why not go straight home to bed? Pierre would find him there when he got back; or, if not then, the next morning.

But he couldn't bring himself to do this. He *had* to see Pierre at the earliest possible moment. He crossed the lock, threw the door open, and saw the café crowded with Pierre's friends. The air was thick with smoke and brandy fumes.

"Hey! There's Charles," someone called.

˗He pushed through the crowd, looking for his brother, whom he found leaning on the counter. His eyes were rather hazy.

"Come on, Charles," he bawled. "Lesh have a squint at you!"

The numerous drinks forced on him had taken their effect, and Pierre caught his brother in his arms dramatically and gave him a loud accolade on each cheek.

"Now, you rascal, tell us what you've been up to all this time."

Charles made a wry face; he couldn't help it. The truth was, once more he felt like weeping. Choking down a sob, he looked at Babette, who was surrounded by a noisy group and seemed to be enjoying herself thoroughly.

"I've just come from Dieppe."

"Give him a drink, Babette."

As he took the glass, he heard in memory her voice: "I know you're going to do something silly—again!"

He smiled. None of the others could understand that smile; it was his secret. Nor had they ever seen him putting down the drinks as he now began to—as fast as they were handed him. The truth was that he'd accepted, once and for all, the present situation. Things were as they were, and it was no use trying to change them. He couldn't have found words for his new attitude toward life, but he was poignantly conscious of it at the back of his mind.

Pierre would have to go on being . . . just Pierre. And that was why he, Charles, must resume his old role, go back to his job at the station first thing in the morning, and when his day's work ended, come and sit here at a corner table, to watch Babette and wait till she had a moment off to come and talk with him.

No doubt Jules would go on giving him ironic glances. Or perhaps Jules, too, had understood . . . ? No, that wasn't probable. But, for Charles, the tangle of his life had sorted itself out into a kind of pattern; he could now see things comprehensively—as from a mountaintop.

181

Even in his rather fuddled state, Pierre looked as handsome as ever. And he showed no sign of being sick, didn't talk nonsense, or fumble for his words. The only changes were his exceptional loquacity and a far-away look in his eyes. . . .

CHARLES WOKE with a splitting headache. Going to the kitchen, he found his mother there, trying to turn the coffee mill without making a noise. Her eyes brimming with tenderness, she pointed to Pierre's room.

"Ssh! He's still asleep."

So Charles, too, made as little noise as possible getting into his railway uniform and, some minutes later, when closing the hall door.

He started out a little earlier than usual. Though the rain looked like it was holding off, it was a sunless morning. A new day was beginning, just an ordinary day, like any other.